The Mystery of Wickworth Manor

Also by Elen Caldecott

How Kirsty Jenkins Stole the Elephant
How Ali Ferguson Saved Houdini
Operation Eiffel Tower

THE Mystery OF WICKWORTH MANOR

ELEN CALDECOTT

BLOOMSBURY

LONDON BERLIN NEW YORK SYDNEY

Bloomsbury Publishing, London, Berlin, New York and Sydney

First published in Great Britain in July 2012 by Bloomsbury Publishing Plc
50 Bedford Square, London, WC1B 3DP

A CIP catalogue record for this book is available from the British Library

ISBN 978 1 4088 2048 3

Typeset by Hewer Text UK Ltd, Edinburgh
Printed in Great Britain by Clays Ltd, St Ives Plc, Bungay, Suffolk

1 3 5 7 9 10 8 6 4 2

www.bloomsbury.com
www.elencaldecott.com

To Simon

PROLOGUE

CJTE/003 Dog's Tooth Pendant, 18th C.

Maggie went to the healer's hut late late at night. The salt of the sea was close, but the sweetness of the sugar canes was closer. Both made the sweat on her skin feel sticky.

She knocked gently. The dune grasses whispered a warning; a golden plover whistled in alarm.

The door opened.

'Yes, daughter?'

'My boy leaves on the tide,' she said. 'I want a charm for him. I want him to be free. Can you help me?'

The man in the doorway grinned. His smile was more gaps than teeth, though the necklace he wore was more teeth than gaps. 'What about the preacher you been talking with? He'd say you be dancing with the devil.'

Maggie stepped into the open doorway. 'I want my son to come back a free man in this world, not in the next.'

CHAPTER 1

Paige Owens slapped a tarot card down on the back seat of the bus. She whistled.

'What?' Sal asked, her dark eyes worried. 'What is it?'

Jo leaned over the seat, eager for a better look.

'Ze Tower,' Paige said in her best Dracula accent. 'Most mysterious.'

The card showed a tall, white building. Tongues of flame shot from its windows and a bolt of lightning slashed the dark sky above it.

'Is that bad?' Sal asked.

'Zis means change, havoc,' Paige answered. 'Like an earthquake shaking up your world. Nothing will ever be ze same again.' She grinned. 'You know, like on the telly when they come and redo your whole house in an hour.'

Jo laughed, but Sal still looked unhappy. 'Well, the cards have got that right. Nothing's the same now.'

'It's good,' Jo said. 'Change is good. Isn't it, Paige?'

Paige didn't answer. She looked outside. The bus had pulled off the main road and was crunching its way up a gravel drive. Willow trees dripped on either side and black yews stood guard, blocking the sunlight. Then the bus came to a stop. Paige tidied up her cards and put them back in their box. 'OK. Paparazzi faces on – we're here.'

Out of one window, Paige could see Wickworth Manor Activity Centre. It was an old house with huge columns across the front, like the bank in *Mary Poppins*. Its windows were as black and shiny as businessmen's shoes. On the other side of the bus, she could see an oval lake. The water twinkled gold with sunshine.

'Maybe there'll be four-poster beds,' Sal said. Her fear hadn't quite gone, but Paige could see that she was doing her best to ignore it.

'Yes, or maybe we'll be sleeping in the attics with the rats,' Jo suggested.

Paige gave her a small punch on the arm. 'Don't frighten Sal.'

'Sorry, Sal. If there are rats, I'll guard you from them.'

Theirs wasn't the only bus. Three more buses spilled children from other schools. Their time in Year 6 was nearly over. In September, all the children here would start their new secondary school together. The idea was they would spend this week getting to know each other so the first few days at secondary school were less scary. Paige grinned. She wasn't scared of secondary school. She wasn't scared of anything. Well, maybe snakes. And spiders. And rats. And perhaps heights. Well, definitely heights. But nothing else. And definitely not secondary school.

She looked at the crowd. Boys and girls shouted, or jumped up and down the steps, or clambered on the stone banisters. It was all colour and movement, like beads bouncing from a broken necklace.

Miss Brown stood up. 'Before you all descend to join in the bedlam, I want to remind you that you are here representing Friar's Street Primary. So no nonsense. Yes, I'm looking at you girls.' She raised a steely eyebrow in Paige's direction. 'Stay to one side, stay together. And anyone who gets run over by a bus will have me to answer to.'

Paige raised an eyebrow right back. If there was a sarcasm Olympics, Miss Brown would take gold, silver and bronze – but she was all right, really.

It was hard to hold a paparazzi face in the blistering heat, but Paige, Sal and Jo did their best, smiling and waving at everyone and giggling the whole time.

5

'Listen *carefully*,' Miss Brown said. 'When I read out your name, take your bag up to the room you've been allocated. Leave your luggage there, then come back downstairs to the hall. Follow the signs.'

Miss Brown yelled out her list. Paige, Sal and Joanne were together in a room called Bluebell right at the top of the house.

'Yay! We're sharing.' Sal sounded relieved.

'Result,' Jo said.

Just before they passed through the front door, Paige looked back at the drive. A silver car, long and sleek, rolled up. It was silent in the middle of the hubbub. It was the kind of silence that reminded Paige of getting a bubble of water in her ear after swimming, sort of wrong and uncomfortable. She swallowed quickly. A boy got out of the car. He wore dark trousers and a blue shirt. His skin was deep brown and his hair was trimmed short. He looked towards Paige and even at this distance she could tell he was frowning. A shiver ran right the way up her spine to the back of her head. Someone walking over her grave.

CHAPTER 2

Curtis Okafor closed the door of his mother's hire car and rested his hand on the roof. The air felt humid and sticky after the chill of the air conditioning inside.

His mother switched off the ignition. 'Do you want me to come in with you?'

Curtis looked towards the house. Wickworth Manor was Georgian, neoclassical; its elegant Doric columns were mottled green with age. It was impossible to see the facade properly because of the buses and the throng of people in the way. He noticed a blonde girl in a blue tracksuit looking at him from the top of the steps. What was she staring at? He turned away, towards the lake and shielded his eyes against the glare of reflected sunlight.

The lake was lozenge-shaped. There was a chapel perched on the bank on the far side. On the nearside a phalanx of canoes were moored against a jetty. No doubt he would be forced into one of those at some point this week.

'Curtis?' his mother asked again. 'Shall I come inside with you?'

He turned back to the car. 'No, thank you. I can manage. No one else has their parents here.'

She nodded once and then popped the boot open. Curtis lifted out his suitcase and went to his mother's side of the car.

They looked at each other.

'I'll be back to collect you in seven days,' she said. 'Ring us if you need anything. Ring anyway, just to tell us how you're settling in.' She paused and gripped the wheel. 'Give it a chance, OK?'

Curtis nodded. His mouth was dry.

Mum was looking towards him, but not at him. 'Curtis –'

'Yes?'

'We love you,' she said as carefully as if she were handling explosives.

He nodded in reply, then clicked up the handle of his suitcase and turned towards the house without another word. He heard the soft purr of the car's engine, then the crunch as she pulled away; he paused, but didn't look back. He ignored the ache in his chest and walked into Wickworth Manor.

8

The hallway of the house was busy: teachers with clipboards rattled out instructions to their groups; pupils grabbed cases and bags, jostling and pushing up the staircase like commuters on a rush hour tube train. Curtis stood still. He knew he should smile, maybe say hello, but his mouth was set in a hard line and every muscle in his face seemed to be set tight. No one jostled him, but no one looked at him either.

Within a few minutes, the hallway emptied. All the pupils had been marshalled up to their rooms and all the noise migrated up into the body of the house. He was on his own.

Suddenly, he felt foolish. Why hadn't he asked someone where to go? Why hadn't he just taken a deep breath and forced himself to talk to someone? He pressed his hand to his chest; the ache was still there. Everyone had just assumed he was with someone else, but he wasn't, he was on his own. He wasn't at Northdene School any more. He pushed the thought away. He wasn't going to stand here feeling sorry for himself.

He grabbed his suitcase and marched up the sweeping staircase; the dorms must be up there. A grandfather clock ticked loudly; behind a closed door someone shouted. He walked on, following the stairs up and up and up. The staircase narrowed at each landing, but sounds came from behind every door. He just needed somewhere quiet; a room with no one in it where he could collect his thoughts. Finally he found himself at the top of the house. The ceiling sloped towards the eaves, sunlight poured in through dormer windows and dust motes danced in the warmth.

A door slammed open and a blonde girl tumbled out. 'Oh,' she said, stopping abruptly. 'It's you.'

Curtis frowned. 'Do I know you?'

'I'm Paige. Do you know your aura is red and swirly? That's not good, you know.'

'My aura?' Curtis asked.

'I'm psychic. Well, training to be.'

'There's no such thing.'

'Fine, Curtis Okafor, suit yourself.'

Curtis's eyes opened wide. How did she know his name? She *couldn't* be psychic. The idea was ridiculous.

'Ha! Your face! Don't worry, your name's written on your suitcase label.' The girl grinned. 'We're meant to be in the hall. You coming?'

Curtis opened his mouth, but no words came out.

She shrugged. 'Doing a goldfish impression? Fine. You're a bit weird, you know that?' She stepped past him and headed for the stairs. Was she giggling?

The psychic thought *he* was weird.

This place was *nothing* like Northdene.

And yet, there was something about the way the light fell across the old floorboards; something about the smell of warm plaster walls and food cooking floors below that made this part of the house feel safe.

Curtis followed the corridor to the end, right to the last door. If this room was empty, he was staying here.

He turned the handle and stepped inside.

It took a moment for his eyes to adjust to the gloom. Heavy curtains were pulled across the window. Slowly, the dark shapes and shadows turned into objects: a bank of filing cabinets, spilling paper; chairs stacked haphazardly, their legs sticking out like broken twigs; a cupboard with a door missing and, against one wall, an old bed. It wasn't a bedroom, it was a room where people dumped the things they didn't need any more. Curtis smiled, without humour.

This would suit him fine.

He could stay here and hide and not have to speak to anyone or explain anything to strangers. He could stay here and eat the biscuits in his suitcase and drink rainwater. He could sleep for seven days and when Mum came to collect him he would tell her what a brilliant time he'd had and they could drive home again in silence.

Curtis kicked off his shoes and fell back on to the bed.

It made a horrible crunching sound.

Curtis pressed his fingertips to his eyelids. Had he really just broken an antique bed? He was pretty certain that he had.

He opened his eyes and rolled off. He'd better take a look at the damage.

Underneath the bed it was dark and cluttered with yet more junk: hatboxes, old shoes, even a broken doll. A plank of wood lolled down from the frame, its edge jagged with splinters. That must be what he'd heard snap.

Curtis reached under the bed gingerly and pressed up against the plank. It waggled like a broken bone. He stretched as far as he could; his shoulder ached with the effort. He tried to ease the wood back into place, but it wouldn't realign. Something was jamming it. With his fingers outstretched he could just about touch whatever it was in the way of the plank.

It felt rough – maybe some kind of fabric? It had a square edge, covered in heavy cloth; it felt like an elbow in a sling. He grabbed the edge and tugged. It came loose. A few sharp yanks pulled it away from the bed frame. He sat back on his heels and pulled it clear of the bed.

He unwrapped the cloth. And gasped.

It was a painting, about half a metre high and a bit less wide. He stood up and pulled the curtain a little until a puddle of light fell on to the canvas. A pair of eyes stared at him from inside the gilt frame. The eyes were dark and ferocious. They belonged to a boy with cropped hair and dark skin. He was wearing a bright red coat – some kind of servant's uniform, maybe? Though the boy didn't really look old enough to have a job; he looked about twelve or thirteen. The red coat had bright gold buttons, each one decorated with a map of the world, like tiny, gleaming globes. But it was the eyes that held Curtis's attention. Angry eyes, lost eyes, frightened eyes. Eyes that seemed to be looking at him as much as he was looking at them.

CHAPTER 3

The welcome speeches were Boredom, Dull Street, Yawnsville. Miss Brown told them to behave; teachers from the other schools told them to behave; the owner of Wickworth Manor told them to behave. Paige rolled her eyes at Sal and Jo; they both giggled.

Then Miss Brown totally ruined everything.

'You will be working in groups,' she said, 'and you'll be assigned a partner within your group for the duration of the week. That way you'll get to know each other better. And therefore, the transition to senior school might not be so mortally terrifying. The groups are arranged alphabetically, by surname.'

Saleema Bibi's and Joanne Cartwright's names were called out in the first group.

Paige looked at Sal and Jo in horror. The two of *them* were together while *she* was lumped in with

14

all the Oates and Osbournes at the other end of the alphabet.

'Please, Miss,' she said to Miss Brown moments later. 'It's not fair. I don't need to meet anyone else. I've got Sal and Jo. They're my mates.'

Miss Brown peered over her clipboard. 'You are here to make new friends, Paige. What would be the point of keeping all the schools separate, hmm?'

'I don't mind about other schools being here. So long as I'm with Sal and Jo.'

'Well, you'll just have to struggle on like the rest of us, Paige. Grin and bear it. It's only for seven days. You'll see them in the evenings.'

Paige glared as the first group was led out of the hall.

Her own group, the 'O's to 'S's, were gathering together. She knew a few of them from Friar's Street and a couple more from around the estate. But none of them were Sal or Jo.

'Now,' Miss Brown said, 'you're with one of the other teachers this week. Mr Appleton. Follow him and find your partner.'

'Who's my partner?' Paige's voice sounded sulky, even to herself.

Miss Brown looked at her clipboard. 'Curtis Okafor. Go and join your group.' Mr Appleton vaguely counted heads. 'Is this everyone?' he asked mildly.

Paige stuck up her hand. 'No. My partner's not here. I think he's lost.'

'Ah,' Mr Appleton sighed. 'Waifs and strays already? Well, go and see if you can find her –'

'Him,' Paige interrupted.

'– and bring her back. Meet the group in Art.'

Paige was about to say that she didn't know where Art was, but Mr Appleton was already leading the group out.

Fine.

She would find the stupid boy and she would find the stupid Art class. And then she would talk to Miss Brown about swapping groups.

Paige stomped along the corridor that led back to the entrance hall. She sprinted up the huge staircase. Mum always said that the best place to look for something was where you left it. He'd been hanging around the top floor earlier. With any luck, he'd still be there.

CHAPTER 4

Curtis propped the painting up against the sturdy wood of the headboard and opened the curtains a fraction more. Now the lustrous shine on the oil paints was clearer, brighter. He sat at the end of the bed, with his knees drawn up to his chin. The painting wasn't signed, but the year had been painted in the bottom right corner – 1805. He let his eyes roam over the surface, noticing the gleam of a button, the weave of the fabric, the crinkle of hair.

Who was this boy?

What had a black boy been doing here in 1805?

Were there even black people in Britain that long ago? Jane Austen was around then and there weren't any in her books. Not that he'd read them, only seen adaptations on television, but still.

Curtis felt interested in something for the first time

in a long time. The ache in his chest seemed to ease a little.

Suddenly, the door banged open behind him. He jumped, then spun round on the bed to see who had opened it.

A girl flounced in. The psychic. Even in his head the word sounded ludicrous. He frowned.

'Here you are!' she said.

Curtis just stared at her. What was her name? Poppy? Pippa? No, Paige, that was it.

'I've been looking everywhere for you,' she said. 'You've got Art with Mr Appleton. Why aren't you there? You'll need to find a new partner, by the way. I won't be staying. Is this your room? This isn't a bedroom. It's full of junk. They didn't put you in here, did they? That's a bit mean of them.'

Curtis wasn't sure which question to answer. So he didn't answer any of them.

'Cat got your tongue?' Paige came over to the bed. 'What are you doing up here anyway?' Her eyes flicked around the room: bed, window, him, bed – like a flea hopping through a pack of dogs. Then they rested on the painting.

She whistled softly. 'Who is that?'

There was a pause. She appeared to be giving him a chance to speak. 'I'm not sure. I just found it,' Curtis said. He moved between Paige and the painting, blocking her view. '*I* found it,' he repeated.

'All right. Keep your hair on.' She stepped to the right and reached around him. Her fingers stretched towards the painting. She was going to touch the canvas.

'Wait!' Curtis said.

BANG!

Both their heads whipped towards the source of the noise. A broom had clattered to the ground, hitting the side of a filing cabinet on its way down.

'Oh,' Paige said softly, looking first at Curtis, then back at the painting. 'Oh, oh, oh! I bet I know who this is.'

'You do?'

Paige's voice dropped to a sibilant whisper. 'This is the Wickworth Boy.'

'Who?'

'You don't know about the Wickworth Boy?'

'No.'

'Well, budge up and I'll tell you.' Paige edged on to the bed, forcing him to move up. She leaned in close; her green eyes were open so wide that he could see the whites around her irises. 'My cousin Chantelle came here two years ago, when she was in Year 6,' Paige said. 'She heard all about him and she told me and Sal and

Jo. When Sal heard she almost refused to come. Took us ages to persuade her.

'Anyway. Once, a long time ago, there was a servant at Wickworth Manor. A boy. And the family who lived here then had a kind and beautiful daughter. Well, the servant boy fell in love with the daughter. And he was so handsome that she fell in love with him right back. They met in secret. But one day her father found out. He was furious. Steaming. He packed his daughter off to a nunnery. Then, he took the servant boy to the dungeon. And that boy was never seen *alive* again. His ghost walks the corridors of the manor, searching for the girl he lost.' Paige sat back, a wicked grin on her face.

'It's a good story,' Curtis said. 'But it's just a story. Made up. Fiction. There won't be any dungeons here, the house is too young.'

Paige raised her eyebrow. 'You don't believe me?' She pointed to the broom. 'What was that then? The broom just fancied seeing what the view was like from down there?'

'No, but perhaps two people coming in here, one of them like a whirlwind, disturbed the air and destabilised the broom. Perhaps it was Chaos Theory.'

'What?' Now Paige sounded scornful.

Curtis wondered whether he should explain Chaos Theory to her. The complex and intricate idea that actions could reverberate and echo in quite unexpected ways, influencing events far from their original source. He looked at her raised eyebrow. He wasn't even going to try to explain. 'There's no such thing as ghosts. And that's just a painting of a boy,' he said instead.

'You what? Of course there are ghosts. I know loads of people who've seen one. My mum, for starters. She saw a ghost in a hospital once. She told me. Oh, wouldn't it be great if I could tell Mum that I saw a ghost too. And my cousin, Chantelle. She's in Year 8 now. She'd be dead impressed if I told her we'd found the Wickworth Boy.'

'But we haven't,' Curtis said.

Paige leaned in closer. 'Yes, but we could have though.'

Curtis looked at the painting. How long had it been hidden away, trapped inside a bed frame? Ten years? Fifty years? A hundred years? Someone had wanted to get rid of it. They wanted the painting out of their sight, forgotten, like the rest of the junk in this room. So they had boarded it up where no one would ever look. And then he had come along and rediscovered it. He dug his fingers into his palms. The thought of the boy being abandoned here made him angry. It wasn't right. 'I want to know who he *really* is,' Curtis said quietly.

21

'We can do a seance!' Paige said. 'I've read about them in my mum's *Fortean Times* and I've seen it on cable. You can speak to souls trapped between here and the beyond. It'll be cool! I'll have something amazing to tell Mum when I get home.'

'How about something a bit more reliable?' Curtis said. 'Like looking on the internet, or perhaps in the library.'

'Where's the fun in that?' Paige asked. 'Come on, if you don't believe in it, where's the harm?'

Curtis suddenly felt exhausted. He just wanted to lie down on the bed, curl up and forget about everything – Mum, Northdene, all of it. He just wanted peace and quiet and to be left alone.

'Say yes, go on,' Paige said.

If he agreed, would she go away? Curtis sighed, then shrugged: *OK then.*

CHAPTER 5

CJTE/006 - Crew list of the Sandford Frigate, 18th C.

He had never felt so sick before in his life.
Not even when he and the other children on the
plantation had sneaked into the boiling shed and
eaten the sticky sweet molasses until they couldn't
move for gluttony. He had been beaten, like the
others, when they were caught. But it had been
worth it. The taste had been so good. Maggie, his
mother, had looked at the red stripes across his
hands and said that soon enough he'd grow to hate
the very smell of the sugar canes.

But he had not grown to hate the canes. His life
had taken another direction. Eastwards. Across the
ocean. For he was on a sailboat and the swell and
break of the sea had turned his skin ashen and
his stomach inside out. Wherever it was they were
heading, as long as the land stayed still, it had
to be better than the sea.

CHAPTER 6

A seance! Paige leapt up off the bed. This was going to be cool. She and Mum often watched *Ghost Finders* curled up together on the sofa with a tub of ice cream. It was their favourite programme. And now, there was an actual real live ghost to look for. Though there was the whole of the rest of the day to get through first. 'Come on, we're meant to be in Art,' she said.

By the time that they managed to find Art – it was hidden in a courtyard at the back of the house in some old barn – the session was pretty much over. Mr Appleton looked a tiny bit cross as they walked in but Paige just beamed at him.

There was the beginning of a wicker structure in the middle of the room; it looked like a very leaky boat. Around it, everyone was packing away and clearing up snipped tissue paper. She picked up a few stray pencils that had rolled on to the floor. It was always a good idea to look helpful when teachers were cross with you.

Suddenly, the back of her neck tingled. It was a feeling she knew. Only last week she and Mum had spent the afternoon practising their sixth sense. One of them would close their eyes and try to feel whether the other was staring at them or not.

So Paige had a pretty good idea what the tingling on her neck meant.

She whipped her head round and caught Liam O'Brian staring at her. He half smirked, half grinned.

'What?' she asked. 'What's so funny?'

Liam lived on her estate, but Mum didn't like her having anything to do with him. His big brother was always getting into trouble with the police.

'Nothing,' Liam said. 'Just wondering where you found your new boyfriend.'

Curtis gasped beside her. Did he have no sense? Reacting to Liam was like waving a red rag to a bull, then kicking it on the shins for good measure: bound to end badly. 'Just ignore him,' she whispered. She raised her chin and said loudly to the room, 'Some people just aren't worth bothering about.'

Liam snorted. With phlegm.

She tugged Curtis's arm and followed the swell of people heading towards the hall. What had he gasped for? Did he want Liam to pick on him? Paige was even more sure, if she hadn't been already, that Curtis was one DVD short of a box set.

The hall had been rearranged after the boring speeches earlier. The wooden floor was hidden by rows of tables and chairs. Grey racks of cutlery and towers of trays were set out near the door. A queue of people stood in front of a serving hatch. Food. Her stomach rumbled. She just hoped there was a good vegetarian option, like pizza.

'Paige!' Sal waved from the queue. 'Guess what? We did archery. With real arrows. I nearly shot the teacher.'

'I hit the board, but not the middle of the target,' Jo added.

Paige walked towards them. Curtis trailed behind her like a lost dog. 'Well,' Paige grinned. 'We found the Wickworth Boy.'

'No!' Sal's eyes flashed wide.

Jo grabbed Paige's arm and pulled her closer. 'You did what?'

'Hey, you can't push in,' a voice said.

Paige glared at the boy who'd spoken.

He shrugged. 'Well, you can't, can you? It isn't fair.'

'Fine.' Paige sighed. 'Sal, Jo, keep me a place at your table.'

Paige went to join the back of the queue. So did Curtis. Didn't he have any friends of his own? Paige wondered for a second which school he was from. And why he'd turned up in a car, not a bus. But then she saw a pinned-up menu and the thought went clean out of her head.

'Salad?' Sal asked, wrinkling her nose.

Paige put down her tray. The salad was already wilting in the heat. 'It was that or burgers. Sal, Jo, this is Curtis. Curtis, sit down.'

'Hi, Curtis,' Sal smiled shyly.

'Tell us about the ghost,' Jo said, biting into her bun. 'It's the one Chantelle told us about. Remember? We found a painting of him in Curtis's room. And then there was a spirit manifestation.'

'A broom fell over,' Curtis said.

'A broom?' Sal giggled.

'It was a manifestation!' Paige rapped the table with her fist. Why was he being so difficult? 'And tonight, we're going to hold a seance.'

'We are?' Jo wriggled with excitement.

Sal looked a lot less happy.

'Yes, we are.' Paige thought about *Ghost Finders*. 'We need supplies. I've seen it on telly. We'll need a candle, and some incense and a table.' Paige looked around the room. 'We can't take a table from here, they're too big.' She looked over her shoulder at Curtis. 'Hey, there are all those broken ones in your room. They'd do.'

'I've got some perfume,' Jo said. 'It isn't incense, but it's what Mum wears to church. I've borrowed it from her.'

'Fine. So, we just need a candle then. Where will we get that from?'

No one answered. They just looked at each other. There was probably a rule book somewhere that said Year 6s weren't allowed candles. At least not to hold seances with anyway.

Then Curtis spoke. 'Does it have to be real?'

'I don't know,' Paige said. 'What else could it be?'

'Well, I've got an app on my phone. It looks like a candle.' He looked a bit embarrassed. 'I use it like a nightlight. You set it off and it burns down until it goes out.' He shrugged. 'I like it.'

'Perfect,' Paige said. 'So, tonight we'll speak to the spirits of the dead.'

CHAPTER 7

Curtis lay across the foot of his bed. It was dark now, though the temperature hadn't dropped much. He hadn't bothered to turn on the ceiling light; he wasn't even sure whether it worked. Instead he had his phone. On the screen a simple white candle burned with an orange flame. It was bright enough for him to make out the colours of the objects nearby: the beige mattress, the green towel he was using as a pillow and the gold frame of the painting propped against the headboard. The rest of the room was in shadow.

The Wickworth Boy.

There was no such thing.

This portrait was something else. It was real. Dumped like junk. Why?

Curtis wanted to know. He wasn't sure why it felt so important, but it did.

He minimised the candle on his phone. Now the only light came from the glow of the icons on the screen. The face of the boy in the painting was plunged into darkness.

He opened the internet browser. He could Google 'Wickworth Manor' and find out whether anyone knew about the boy. That was more likely to produce results than any weird seance or tea leaf reading or other daft idea that Paige might come up with.

Oh.

There was no 3G coverage, or Wi-Fi. Still, there must be an internet connection somewhere in the house. There had to be: you couldn't run an activity centre without email, surely? He would look for it as soon as he had a chance.

His finger hovered over his phone. He paused. He might not have internet coverage, but the bars showed that the phone was working just fine. The ache in his chest that had been dormant all afternoon suddenly blossomed. People could call him, if they wanted. Mum and Dad could call.

But they hadn't.

He remembered the sound of Mum's car pulling away earlier in the day. Had she looked back at him in her mirror? Had she waved, or blown a kiss? She had on his first day at Northdene. On that day he had stood watching her leave, waving and waving until his arm felt sore. And she had waved right back, until the car pulled out of sight. He had felt so hopeful then, his heart swollen with the possibility of it all. He had been sure that he would be a star pupil, a hero at sports, a leader.

And now look at him.

In an attic, hiding from everyone, with a pretend candle for company. And Northdene was over, he would never see it again and it was all his own fault. Mum knew that. No wonder she hadn't rung.

He closed his eyes. He should get into his pyjamas, but he felt too tired to move. He lay still and silent in the sticky heat.

Gentle tapping roused him. Tapping and giggling.

They were here for their stupid seance. He stood up and marched over to the door. He opened it a crack and peered out into the corridor. Paige, Sal and Jo stood there in pyjamas and dressing gowns, slippers on their feet and grins on their faces. Sal even appeared to be holding a stuffed bear, as if this was a slumber party. Curtis frowned. 'You can't come in,' he said.

'Why? Aren't you decent?'

'Yes, of course I am. I just think it's a stupid idea. If we want to know more about the portrait, then we need to do proper research. Find out who painted it and why, things like that.'

Paige leaned on the door. It eased open a few centi-metres and she ducked down under his arm. He was forced to step back, otherwise she'd barge right into him. Sal and Jo slipped in too.

'This *is* research,' Paige said. 'Very important research. Stop moaning. Can I turn the light on? Just while we set up.' Without waiting for an answer, she flicked the switch. A wan bulb lit up in the centre of the ceiling.

'Is this him?' Sal whispered. She and Jo were by his bed, looking at the painting.

'It's cool, isn't it?' Paige said. 'The Wickworth Boy. A tortured soul looking for revenge for his stolen love.'

'You don't know that,' Curtis said.

Paige ignored him. 'Jo, help me with this table. Sal, we need some chairs. You, Curtis, bring the paint-ing closer. Put it on a chair. We need to channel our energy towards it.' She was busy clearing archive boxes from the top of an old desk. Jo helped her drag it into the centre of the floor. Sal found a few chairs that seemed safe enough to sit on, even if they were a bit wobbly.

'I think the portrait's better on the bed,' Curtis said. 'Those chairs look like they might collapse.'

Paige rolled her eyes. 'Fine. We'll just have to chan-nel our energy a bit further. Put your candle on the table. Jo, can you put a bit of perfume around the place, for incense? Sal, we're ready, turn off the light.'

There was something about Paige that was like the tide coming in, or a bulldozer on a demolition site – something impossible to stop. She just didn't come with brakes.

The three of them took their seats around the table and looked at him expectantly. He sighed. The sooner he did this, the sooner they would go away and leave him in peace. He sat.

For a while nothing seemed to be happening. He put his palms flat on the table top, like the others. In the fake candlelight the colours of their hands looked like some cheesy, world-as-one advert: black, brown, peach and pale. The flame on the screen flickered gently.

'Everyone, breathe deeply,' Paige said.

Curtis heard their lungs fill and the air flow as they exhaled. Slow, regular sounds. He found himself copying their breathing, even though he didn't really want to.

'Empty your mind,' Paige said. 'Feel your chi gathering inside of you. Feel your energy building. Then, send that energy out towards the Wickworth Boy.' Her voice dropped deeper, 'Spirits, we call on you. Is there anyone there?'

Sal giggled. Then gasped. Paige must have kicked her under the table.

'Spirits, can you hear us? Give us a sign.'

The sounds of the house seemed amplified in the darkness: downstairs a door banged; above them something in the eaves rustled; outside a night bird called. Curtis looked at Paige. Shadows were cast upwards over her face; her eye sockets were black, as though her eyes had fallen inwards. Her lips moved, silent but rapid, as though she were speaking an incantation. Beside him, Jo's hand grabbed his and squeezed tightly. He could see anticipation in her eyes.

'Spirits, if you are there, speak to us!'

A sudden bang made them all jump.

Sal yelped.

Paige's eyes flashed open.

'What was that?' Jo asked.

Curtis looked around; nothing in the room had been disturbed. The sound had come from outside.

'I can feel something coming. A presence,' Paige said.

'I don't like it,' Sal said quietly. Then, a little louder, 'I don't like it.'

'It was just a car backfiring, or something like that,' Curtis said.

'It's getting closer,' Paige said. 'Closer. The spirits are nearly here. They come to share their secrets. Focus, everyone! Listen!'

There were footsteps outside; heavy in the corridor. They moved quickly, coming towards them. Curtis felt his throat constrict and his mouth go dry.

The door leapt open.

'What on earth is going on in here?' a voice said.

CHAPTER 8

'*I said*, what is going on in here?'

Paige knew the woman in the doorway from somewhere, but it took a second to remember who she was
– Mrs Burton-Jones, the owner of Wickworth Manor.
She had been one of the ones going on about good
behaviour when they'd first arrived. Oops.

Now she stood glaring at them like an angry bull in
a flowery dressing gown.

'Nothing's going on,' Paige said.

Mrs Burton-Jones's face seemed to swell, like a bull
turning into a frog. 'Clearly not nothing,' she yelled. 'I
do my final rounds for the night. I discover that Bluebell
is empty and then I find that you are conducting some
kind of voodoo. Or witchcraft. Or devil worship!'

Paige stood up. 'Hang on,' she said. 'We weren't
doing any harm. It isn't witchcraft. Or if it is, it's white

witchcraft. We just heard there were ghosts, that's all.' Her eyes flicked towards the bed. The painting was in darkness. Mrs Burton-Jones hadn't turned on the light. And it had to stay that way.

Paige sprang up and moved towards the doorway. Mrs Burton-Jones was forced to step back into the corridor.

'Honest,' Paige said, following Mrs Burton-Jones, 'we didn't mean any harm. It was just a laugh.'

She could hear the others moving inside the room. She hoped one of them had the sense to move the painting out of sight. Curtis would, he had brains. Probably.

'This is no laughing matter, young lady.' Mrs Burton-Jones's eyes bulged out of their sockets. 'This is my home that you are desecrating. The Burton-Joneses have lived here for generations. I will not stand for such appalling behaviour in this house. You have let yourselves down, and you have let your school down. Which school are you with?'

Paige felt a sinking feeling. Great. Now Miss Brown would get involved and be sarcastic all over the place. 'Friar's Street,' she said.

'I should have known.'

'Hey,' Paige said, 'what's that supposed to mean?'

'That's enough. All of you, get to your rooms, right now. You'll hear more about this in the morning. You *and* your teachers. Go!'

They had no choice.

Paige moved aside to let Sal, Jo and Curtis file out. As she closed the door she glanced into the room. They had been so close, she was certain of it. Their energy was still strong; she could almost see it, like a heat haze around the table. *We won't give up*, she told the spirit, *we'll speak to you somehow.*

CHAPTER 9

Mrs Burton-Jones herded them like sheep down the corridor, sniping at them with every step. The girls ducked into Bluebell so that Curtis was left alone with Mrs Burton-Jones.

He kept walking. Where would he go? If he told this woman that he hadn't found his dorm yet, she would be furious. She'd march him to wherever he was meant to be staying; everyone there would wake up and think he was an idiot.

He couldn't handle that again. He couldn't walk down school corridors thinking that everyone was pointing at him behind his back, whispering about him. The whole point of being here was to try again. A new start, Mum had called it.

Some start.

Where was he going? Curtis looked at the doors as

they passed them, solid, polished wood, each with a plaque bearing the name of a flower. And then one with a different plaque – a stick man.

Curtis stopped walking. 'Excuse me, Ma'am, I'm sorry for causing such a fuss. I will go straight back to my room. But I need to use the bathroom first.'

Mrs Burton-Jones frowned at him and then hid a yawn with the back of her hand. 'Fine. We'll each have more to say about this in the morning. I expect to see you in my rooms downstairs first thing after breakfast. Any more nonsense tonight and you will be heading straight back home, have I made myself clear?'

Curtis waited in the bathroom until he was sure that Mrs Burton-Jones was gone. It was only a temporary reprieve. Tomorrow, he would have to go and face her again. He hadn't even managed one night without getting into trouble.

What would Mum and Dad think if they found out? Dad would look disappointed. Mum would try and hide her tears. Again.

This was all Paige's fault. She was trouble.

Back in the attic room, he climbed into bed, careful not to knock over the painting. He pulled his jacket over himself for a blanket and fell into a restless sleep.

*   *   *

When morning came, he dressed quickly and went downstairs. As he crept past Bluebell, he heard nothing. Good. He was going to stay as far away from Paige as possible. He had found the painting by himself and he would find out about the boy by himself too. He didn't need anyone.

Breakfast was in the main hall. It was already filling up and groups of children chattered and laughed and greeted each other. There was no sign of Paige and the others.

Curtis filled a cereal bowl at the counter, then turned to face the room.

Suddenly, there was a cold feeling in his belly. There were no empty tables. He was going to have to sit down next to someone. He glanced around. A group of girls had their heads close together, whispering to one another. A couple of boys were talking loudly in what sounded like Polish. Another group of boys in loose sports clothes and hoodies ate cornflakes in silence. He recognised one of them from Art yesterday. Liam.

Curtis carried his tray towards the silent boys.

He left a gap of a couple of chairs, then sat down.

The sound of spoons scraping bowls and milk being slurped was loud. But no one spoke.

Then a boy with longish hair brushed to one side of his face leaned towards Curtis. 'What school are you from, then? Friar's?' he asked. The boy jabbed his spoon in the air for emphasis.

'Actually, I'm from Northdene Prep, but I won't be attending Northdene High.'

The boy laughed. It wasn't very kind laughter. 'Actually, is that right, actually?'

A few of the boys smirked. Curtis felt the blood rise in his cheeks. 'Yes, it is.'

'And did you bring your valet with you? Or your nanny? Which one helped you get dressed?' The boy bashed knuckles with the person sitting next to him. A current of laughter ran around the table.

Curtis stared down at his bowl.

'Maybe his chauffeur helped?' a fat boy with a black T-shirt said.

'Or his butler?' someone else added.

'Or his slave?'

'Good one,' Liam said. Their laughter sounded ugly.

Curtis concentrated on the yellow flakes turning to mush on his spoon. He wasn't hungry any more.

'Good morning!' a bright voice said.

He looked up. Paige.

He looked down again.

'Not a morning person?' She put her tray down. 'Neither is my mum. She says I rabbit on worse than daytime telly. Usually she likes it, but not before she's had her morning tea.' She sat down. 'Sal and Jo are on their way. But listen,' her voice dropped to a whisper, 'we all need to get our story straight.'

Curtis didn't answer.

'We all have to go and get told off this morning, remember?'

'Of course I remember.'

'Good. I thought you were giving me the silent treatment for a minute. Oh, here they are.'

Curtis looked up. Sal and Jo were walking towards the table, arm in arm. Sal looked worried, her dark eyes shiny with emotion. Jo held her chin up, ready for anything. He nodded to them as they squeezed in next to Paige. The three were sat across from him like they were planning on interrogating him.

'So,' Paige said. 'I'll do the talking. I'll say we were just telling each other ghost stories, for fun, and we're really sorry and nothing like that will ever happen again and we've learned our lesson. We don't say anything about the painting or the seance or the Wickworth Boy. How does that sound?'

Curtis shrugged. It sounded like Paige was used to being in trouble.

CHAPTER 10

Paige wasn't worried. Mrs Burton-Jones might have seemed like an angry bullfrog last night, but really, who was at their best in the middle of the night? It was only natural to get a bit freaked out if you thought someone was summoning demons in your house. Paige bet Mrs Burton-Jones was lovely when you got to know her.

'You four children are a menace and a disgrace,' Mrs Burton-Jones said. 'Never in all my days have I been so disgusted.'

Well, maybe she wasn't *lovely*. Maybe she was more *OK*.

'You've shown me that your school is not to be trusted. Hoodlums and vandals, the lot of you.'

All right, maybe she was a bullfrog.

Paige stood with Curtis, Sal and Jo in Mrs Burton-Jones's lounge. It wasn't like the lounge back at home with the flat-screen TV and the squidgy sofa. This room had spindly old furniture and knick-knacks that would break as soon as you looked at them and posh things like a little piano and an old globe.

Mrs Burton-Jones sat on a pale blue sofa. Miss Brown stood beside her – frowning her bad frown.

'What have you got to say for yourselves?'

'We're not vandals,' Paige said. She glanced over at Curtis, who was looking down at his shoes. 'Really. Or hoodlums. We're sorry, Miss. We didn't mean any harm. We were just being daft. Over-excitement, I bet. That's what my mum says about me sometimes. We were being silly, trying to scare each other with ghost stories. But we won't do anything like that again. I promise.'

Miss Brown made a noise that, if she hadn't been a teacher, would have been a snort.

'Well, I should think so too,' Mrs Burton-Jones said. 'I've had trouble from Friar's Street before. But I'd have expected more from a Northdene boy. My sons went there, you know. It's very upsetting.'

Miss Brown's frown became even sterner. 'Yes. Quite. Paige, I don't want to hear another complaint like this again. Do I make myself clear?'

'Yes, Miss.'

'And the same goes for the rest of you. Any more nonsense and you'll be sent straight home.'

Mrs Burton-Jones nodded. 'I'm not sure I shouldn't just send you home this minute, but Miss Brown assures me that this won't happen again.'

'No, Miss,' everyone muttered.

Miss Brown shook her head, then said, 'OK, off you trot.'

In the hallway outside, Paige grinned at Curtis. 'Well, that wasn't too bad.'

His eyebrows furrowed together and his mouth twisted into a scowl. 'Speak for yourself. I'm never letting you get me into something like that again. Just stay away from me, OK?'

He turned away from them and stormed down the corridor. Paige watched him go, then said to Sal and Jo, 'What's up with him? We're not being sent home, are we?'

What was Curtis's problem?

CHAPTER 11

Curtis ignored everyone all morning. It was easy to do; Mr Appleton took them on a nature walk around the grounds. Curtis wrote occasionally in the notebook he'd been given: *oak*, *elder*, *sycamore*, and drew a few rough outlines of leaves. But he wasn't able to concentrate. The heat made his brain feel fuzzy. He kept remembering Mrs Burton-Jones's words: *I'd have expected more from a Northdene boy.*

But he wasn't a Northdene boy. Not any more.

That life was gone. Over.

The minute he had stepped into the headmaster's office and seen the look of disappointment on his face, Curtis had known it was over. He had thought that telling his mum and dad would be the worst part. But it wasn't. The worst part was having to look at them every day, knowing how badly he had let them down.

I'd have expected more from a Northdene boy.

Curtis was glad when Mr Appleton said it was time to go back for lunch.

He let everyone else rush past him into the dining hall. He couldn't face it. He'd just go and hide until it was time for whatever pointless group activity was planned for the afternoon.

He thought he'd go up to his room, maybe find something to read, or play on his phone. He paused halfway up the staircase. Everyone would be at lunch. That meant he had the perfect opportunity to look around the manor. It was the perfect time to search for an internet connection or maybe a library. He wouldn't waste this hour; he'd find out about the boy in the portrait.

There had to be a library somewhere. Country houses all had libraries.

He leapt up the last few steps on to the first landing. Unlike the corridor at the top of the house, where his room was, this was wide, with high ceilings and moulded cornices. This was still the grand part of the house. The perfect place for the library. There were three doors on the south side of the corridor, all marked 'private'. Just his luck. Well, he would just have to be quick and hope he didn't get caught. He glanced up and down the corridor before peeking into the rooms.

Behind the first door, Curtis discovered a music room. The second door revealed a small sitting room.

He found what he was looking for behind the third door. It swung open on silent hinges. Inside, the air smelled of dust and warm pages. He felt his heart rise. The smell of books and summer afternoons.

Three huge windows looked out on to the lake and the chapel in the distance. The other three walls were ranged floor-to-ceiling with books; leather-bound volumes in shades of red, brown and green. He walked into the room, breathing it all in. Then he noticed a computer on a small desk. It was old, with a thick square screen and dust on the keyboard. It was pushed into a corner, as though it had been dumped and forgotten about. Did it even work?

He stepped over to it and switched it on. The screen lit up. Perhaps it had belonged to one of Mrs Burton-Jones's grown-up sons. As he waited for the computer to load, he looked around the shelves. There were books on law and science; a few on philosophy that were written in Latin. They must be really old, perhaps as old as the house itself.

Curtis went back to the computer and sat down. He clicked Internet Explorer and heard a weird clicking sound, like a fax machine. Dial-up? Wow, this really was ancient. The pages were slow to load, as though the computer was waking from a deep sleep. He listened out for any noises from the corridor. It was silent, for now. Still, he had to be quick if he didn't want to get caught. If that was even possible without broadband. He opened a search engine, but Googling 'Wickworth Manor' just brought up information about canoeing holidays and team-building weekends. Useless.

What about the portrait? He tried 'Wickworth portraits', 'painting 1805' and 'black servant picture' but none of the images that loaded – painfully slowly – was the one he was looking for.

He expanded the search. Galleries, museums, history of art, he clicked on link after link. But nothing. This was like looking very slowly for a needle in a mountain-sized haystack. The new page in the notebook beside him remained empty. He sat back in the chair.

Outside, he could hear the sound of a game of football drifting up from the lawn. Everyone must have finished lunch. He didn't have long left.

He turned away from the screen. The books. Were any of them about Wickworth Manor? He scanned the shelves. Then his eyes landed on a spine that looked different, out of place. It looked more modern than any of the others. He took a closer look: *Stately Homes of Britain vol. XX.* Aha! Why else would they only have volume twenty and none of the earlier volumes?

Curtis pulled it off the shelf and looked at the contents page. There! *Chapter 6. Wickworth Manor,*

Avon. They'd bought the book that had themselves in it.

"*'Wickworth Manor in Avon,*'" he read, "*'is a fine example of neoclassical architecture. The original house was established in the Tudor period, but was completely redesigned in the late eighteenth century when it was purchased by William Burton. The Burton family came to prominence at that time as leading merchants with wealth generated by West Indian sugar plantations.'*"

Despite the warmth of the sunshine flooding in through the windows, Curtis suddenly felt cold.

Sugar plantations.

Slavery. They'd studied that at Northdene.

He knew that early sugar plantations were worked by slaves; people who were bought and sold like animals. People who were taken from Africa and transported to a new continent, a place where they knew no one and had no family and no hope of returning home. Was that what had happened to the boy in the portrait?

Curtis slumped down to the floor and propped the book against his knees. He felt sick. He took a slow, deep breath and carried on reading:

"*'The family prospered and built the house that stands on the site today, totally demolishing all remnants of the earlier building. But William Burton did not live to enjoy his new palatial home; he died in 1805 following*"

the untimely death of his youngest daughter, Patience, a few weeks earlier. The estate was inherited by his elder daughter, Verity Burton, who died without issue in 1866 at which point it passed to a cousin."'

Curtis skim read the passage again. Then he scribbled quickly in his notebook:

William Burton, a plantation owner, died in 1805.

The portrait was painted in 1805.

Patience Burton, the youngest daughter of the family, died in 1805.

Everything happened in that one year.

Had Paige been right all along with her stupid ghost stories? Had the boy and Patience fallen in love and been killed by William? But then, how had William died? And who hid the painting? And why paint the boy in the first place? There were more questions than answers.

He closed the book. Now he knew how the family had made their money, there was one more thing he had to Google.

He went back to the computer and typed 'slaves in Britain'.

Over three million hits.

He clicked on the first article and read as quickly as he could; a bit about the Romans, the Vikings, the Normans; he scrolled down the page. He slowed down as he reached the eighteenth century and the description of the Triangular Trade. Ships carrying goods sailed from Britain to the west coast of Africa. They traded the goods for slaves, then the slaves were taken to the West Indies and sold to plantation owners. Finally, the ships took sugar and cotton back to Britain – three voyages, three cargoes, three lots of profit. And some of the captains brought personal slaves back to Britain to show off how rich they were.

Black people in servants' uniforms. People who sat on top of their owners' coaches, to show all the neighbours how wealthy the family were. Their boy had the same uniform: livery. Did he decorate the top of the Burtons' coach like the hood ornament on a posh car?

Curtis took another slow breath.

He read the next section carefully, looking at the dates.

In 1807 the Triangular Trade was banned.

In 1832 slavery was abolished in the British Empire.

Their boy, the boy in the painting, in 1805, had he been a slave? Had he been brought to Britain from Africa or the West Indies to be paraded around like a pedigree dog to show everyone just how rich the Burton family was? The idea made him feel sick to his stomach.

It wasn't right.

Curtis switched off the computer. It just wasn't right.

CHAPTER 12

CJTE/009 - Model of the Sandford Frigate, after Pocock.

Land was spotted after nearly two months at sea. The cry came first from the crow's nest atop the main mast. Then the crew and all the passengers stood on the deck to observe the thin streak of grey on the horizon.

Land, at last.

He had found what the crew called his sea legs by the second week. But he would still be glad to walk on solid earth once more. He knew he should go to his master's cabin. There was work to be done. But he stood fast for a while and watched the grey become green.

His mother, Maggie, had prayed for this, with the preacher and with the obeah man. Prayed for her boy to walk on free soil. Word had come, filtered through sailors and overseers, that when a slave stepped on to British soil he became a free man. So, Maggie had let their master, Sir William, take her son as his new manservant.

He looked at his new home. England.

He was ready to take his first free step.

CHAPTER 13

Paige had no idea where Curtis was and she cared even less. He had completely blanked her on the nature walk and he'd vanished at lunchtime. Well, fine. If he was so stuck-up and hoity-toity that he minded getting into a tiny bit of trouble, then she was better off without him.

After dinner time she joined Mr Appleton's group in the courtyard at the back of the house. She noticed Curtis standing at the edge of everyone. He could stay there.

On one side of the courtyard was the Art Barn she'd been in yesterday. Sal and Jo's group were in there now and she could hear everyone chatting as they found their tables.

That wasn't where their group was headed. They were waiting for Mr Appleton to unlock the shed where the ropes were kept. This afternoon, it was climbing. Paige shuddered. If there was anything she hated worse than spiders and rats and snakes combined, it was heights. This was going to be horrible.

Paige took her harness and helmet when the instructor handed it to her. But she wasn't about to put it on. Not unless they forced her to. Mr Appleton looked like Bob the Builder with his yellow hat on. Paige could hear Liam and his mates whispering 'he can fix it' as they tramped around the lake. They were all headed towards a place in the grounds where rocks bulged out of the earth like boils on a plague victim. Paige felt her mouth getting dry.

'Right, equipment on, everyone,' the instructor yelled. Then she went around the group making sure everyone was buckled in right.

The rock was at least twenty metres high. It was browny-grey like a rotten tooth and covered in lumps and cracks that they were supposed to climb up. No danger.

'Problem, Paige?' Mr Appleton asked. Then he chuckled. 'Problem page, ha, like in a magazine.'

Paige glared at him.

'Sorry. Are you having difficulty, Paige?' he asked.

'No. I just don't like heights. I don't want to do this.'

'Oh dear. Well, maybe you should let your partner go first. Where is he? Oh, there. Curtis! Come here. Paige has nominated you to go first. I hope that's OK.'

Curtis looked at them. Paige thought for a moment that he was going to say something, but he just pressed his lips together and stepped over. He pulled his helmet on in silence.

'Sir,' Paige tried again. 'I am not going up there. If God had meant us to climb, we would still be monkeys. But we're not; we're people. Therefore, God didn't mean for us to climb.'

The corner of Mr Appleton's mouth twitched.

'I went up a ladder once,' Paige said. 'I was so scared I froze. Mum had to bribe me back down with mini Mars bars.'

'Well,' Mr Appleton said. 'I'll keep some chocolate on standby, shall I?'

The instructor finished getting everyone ready. The ropes were threaded through metal loops near the top of the rock; one end was meant to be tied to the climber, the other was for their partner to hold. Once the instructor had tied everyone's knots properly and double-checked the harnesses it was time to climb.

Curtis rested his palms on the rock face. 'Don't let me fall,' he said before he lifted himself up.

She nodded. He might be a stuck-up snob, but that didn't mean she'd drop him on his head. Probably. Curtis began to climb. Paige watched him stretch for a handhold, then shift his weight from one leg to another before reaching up again. She had to admit that he was pretty good at it.

Once he was at the top, the instructor came over. 'Right,' she called up to him. 'Hold on to the rope and sit back in your harness.' She took the mechanism from Paige and released it gently. Curtis hopped down the rock as though it was the easiest thing on earth.

'Swap over,' the instructor said, then moved to the next set of climbers.

'That was great!' Curtis said. He was out of breath, but smiling. 'My fingertips are a bit sore, but that was an amazing feeling.'

He seemed to have forgotten his sulk.

'I don't want to,' Paige said.

'I know, I heard all that stuff you said to Mr Appleton.'

'I mean it, I can't do it.'

Curtis untied the rope from his harness and passed it to Paige. She took it, with her fingers trembling. Curtis tied the knot for her. The instructor glanced at it and nodded before moving on.

'You're not scared, are you?' Curtis asked.

Paige felt herself bristle. Of course she was scared. But she didn't want Posh Pants to know that. She found herself moving towards the rock.

She took a big gulp of air and puffed it out again. With one hand on the rock face she stretched upwards and took her feet off the ground. The rope tightened. She felt the tug on the harness around her waist. She paused.

'You're not stopping, are you? Don't be ridiculous,' Curtis said. 'You're only thirty centimetres off the ground. Like standing on a box. Just do what you just did another six or seven times and you'll be at the top.'

The rock was just in front of her nose. She was close enough to see every grain of sand. The brim of her helmet clipped the cliff face and she heard the rasping sound it made, almost a vibration, in her skull. She crept up a little further. There was a bulge of stone an arm-stretch away. She raised her hand slowly. Her palm had a sheen of sweat on it.

'Go on,' Curtis said from below, 'you're taking for ever.'

Around her people had already made it to the top and were dropping down like conkers on strings, plummeting back towards the ground on their thin ropes.

'I can't move,' Paige whispered at the rock.

'What? Of course you can. Just lift your arm, it's not hard.'

'I'm stuck.' Paige could see her knuckles turning white. Her hand was clamped so tightly to the rock that it was as though it had fused there.

She stifled a sob.

And then she felt something awful.

The rock leaned, ever so slightly, towards her. It tipped her backwards.

She gasped.

Her fingers uncurled.

She fell.

Her stomach lurched upwards. Adrenalin shot through her, tingling like a cold shower.

Then she was yanked to a halt. The rope had broken her fall, but now she was dangling three metres above the ground. Her fingers curled around the rope. She closed her eyes and tried to slow her breathing. Curtis was lowering her down. As her feet touched the floor, her knees gave way and she landed in a crumpled heap.

'What was that?' Curtis asked. 'You dropped like a stone.'

Paige sat on the ground, her palms pressed against the earth. They felt cold and clammy, despite the sunshine. 'It wasn't me. It moved,' she whispered.

'What are you talking about?'

'It moved. The rock kind of, well, shrugged.'

Paige looked up, Curtis's face was in shadow; the sun was behind him. But it was still easy to see his look of scorn.

'Look, I know what I felt.' Paige lifted herself up from the ground.

'What you felt was vertigo – it's a sense of disorientation or dizziness. An imbalance of your inner ear. What you did *not* feel was the rock moving.'

'I did.'

'Are you really trying to tell me that the rock decided it didn't want you climbing it? Are you saying rocks have spirits now, as well as paintings and tarot and all the other rubbish you believe in?'

Paige tugged at the knot around her waist, desperate to untie it, to get herself away from the rock face. 'I know what I felt,' she gasped. 'And it isn't rubbish. Who do you think you are anyway? Looking down your nose at us all?'

The rope was finally undone. She flung it to the ground. 'You think you're so much better than us because you went to some snobby school. But you're not there any more, are you? You're here with us.'

Curtis stepped backward. 'That's not . . . that's not what I think.'

'Yes, it is. And I'm sick of it. Don't believe me if you don't want to, but I know what I felt.'

'Is everything OK here?' The instructor was back by their side.

'Yes, Miss,' Curtis said. 'Paige just got a bit . . . I mean, she felt something funny.'

'Hmm, yes, she does look a bit poorly. Sunstroke, maybe? I think you should sit this one out, Paige. Do you want to sit down in the shade?'

Paige nodded. She wasn't going near that rock again. What she had felt was real. The rock hadn't wanted her on it and it had pushed her off. Curtis didn't want to believe that there were things he couldn't understand. He wanted everything neat and clear and straightforward. But the world just wasn't like that. It was obvious that they had disturbed something here. Maybe by moving the painting. They had woken something that had been sleeping for a very long time. Paige sat down in the shadow and drew her knees up to her chin.

If only she could ask Mum what to do.

Her eyes prickled. She suddenly wished that she was back at home, with Mum singing pop songs at the top of her voice while Paige danced around their tiny kitchen. Even if the neighbours did moan about the noise. She'd rather be there, or back at Friar's Street, or mucking about on the estate.

Anywhere but here.

CHAPTER 14

Paige thought he was a snob. And Liam and his friends definitely thought he was. Curtis stood holding the loose end of his rope, alone. He watched Paige sit down in the shade and rest her chin on her knees.

Should he apologise?

No. No way. She was wrong and it would do her no good to have people agree with her just to keep her happy. And it wasn't as though they were friends, even. She'd got him in trouble. She was insensitive and loud and believed in astrology and witches. And she had glitter on her clothes. What was he doing with someone who thought glitter was a fabric?

Curtis climbed twice more with the instructor as his partner. He got to the top both times, but it didn't feel as exhilarating as it had the first time.

The rock couldn't have moved. It was simply impossible. It was a sandstone pillar jutting out of the earth. It was formed of layer upon layer of river bed or flood plain. Millions of years in the making. Things like that didn't move. Well, they didn't *shrug*, anyway. How could she not see that it was in her head?

Eventually, the session was over. The ropes were looped into figures of eight. Helmets came off and harnesses were removed. Curtis looked at the spot where Paige had been sitting. There was no sign of her; she must have gone back to the house.

'Where's your girlfriend?'

Liam.

Great.

'She's not my girlfriend. I hardly know her.'

'You want to steer clear of her,' Liam said. 'She's mental. Her mum's a witch, you know.'

Curtis looked at Liam. He was grinning. Was he serious? Was there no one at this school who didn't believe in fairies and goblins and things that go bump in the night? 'A witch?'

'Yeah. I swear. Not with broomsticks and things. Not like that. A modern witch. People on the estate go to her to read their fortunes. Anyway, I reckon being around all that has made Paige a bit nuts. This is serious advice I'm giving here, bro. You want to get yourself some better mates.' Liam winked.

Curtis shook his head. Had he really just been called 'bro'?

'I think you're all right, you know,' Liam said. 'Some of the boys, they ain't sure, they think that you think you're it. But I said, no, he's just new. It's hard to be the new man.'

Curtis shrugged.

'So, I've decided to give you a chance, yeah? We're going to have a laugh tonight. But we need your help, bro.'

Liam laid a hand on Curtis's arm. Curtis had a strong desire to shrug it off. But he didn't. There was something about the look on Liam's face: listen to me, it said, listen to me or you'll regret it.

'What do you mean, "a laugh"?' Curtis asked. He wished Liam would let go of his shoulder.

Liam gave a small squeeze. 'Right. This place is meant to be haunted, yeah? Well, we were thinking that it would be wicked to make sure it is haunted, just for tonight. We'll set up a ghost and frighten everyone. We'll be a . . . what's it called?'

'A manifestation?' Curtis suggested.

'Yeah, bro, exactly. We'll be ghosts. Frighten everyone.'

'Bedsheets and spooky noises?' Curtis asked, rolling his eyes.

Liam just laughed. 'Something like that. I got some wicked dry ice from my brother.'

Curtis tilted his head to one side. 'Where do I come in?'

'Well, it's your voice, see. No one talks like you talk. You sound proper posh. If any of us sounds like some dead guy from history, it's you. You're going to be the voice of the dead.'

The voice of the dead? Something about those words made Curtis shiver. He pulled his arm free.

Liam spread his hands wide and grinned. 'What? You scared of upsetting the real ghosts?'

'No, of course not.'

'Then what, bro?'

'I don't think it's right, that's all. I don't think you should pretend that kind of thing and scare people. Some people believe in that stuff, you know.'

Liam stopped smiling. He brought his hands down and crossed them in front of his chest. 'Looks like they were right about you, new man. Just remember, I tried to give you a chance, yeah?'

Curtis walked back to the house alone. He felt tired and hungry. His room was stuffy from the heat of the late afternoon sun baking the roof above it. The air tasted like cotton wool. He lay down on his bed. The boy in the painting looked back at him. The slave in the painting? The servant? The status symbol? Curtis didn't know what to call him. He must have had a name. Curtis rubbed his eyes; the lids felt heavy. How was it that someone could live a life and then a few hundred years later, everything about that life had been forgotten? The boy was left with no name, no history, just a painting and some ghost stories.

Curtis realised his eyes were wet. Was that all a life was, when it was over? Just ghost stories?

CHAPTER 15

CJTE/015 Broad Quay, British School, 18th C.

From the docks and the high reek of the sea, the house was half a day's ride. He sat atop the coach, with a driver as sullen and grey as the sky above them. The man beside him held the reins and cursed at the road, the horses, the mud and the boy. His welcome was as warm as two-day-old corn meal.

As they rolled past the quay and the narrow houses of the city, the boy stared. Never before had he seen such pale, awkward creatures as the inhabitants of this place. Their faces were bleached and bloated like some poor drowned thing fished from the brine. They jostled each other and batted their children. They shrieked and cried and stank like sea birds. He was pleased to leave them behind.

He was headed to his master's home. He was headed for his new life.

CHAPTER 16

Curtis woke with a fuzzy head and hunger pains stabbing his stomach. The light in the room was dim. What time was it? He checked his phone: eight o'clock. He had missed dinner and no one had come to wake him. Curtis stretched until he heard his bones clicking. He needed to eat; he hadn't had anything since breakfast. No wonder he was feeling so melancholy. Low blood sugar.

He couldn't be bothered to move just yet.

No one had come to wake him.

No one here had noticed he was missing at dinner and wondered where he was. Paige was the nearest thing he had to a friend and she wasn't talking to him. He pulled his phone out of his case. No missed calls. No one was wondering how he was.

Well. He didn't need them anyway. He threw his phone back. He would find some food for himself.

There would be something edible in the refectory kitchen. Some cheese and bread would be enough. He felt himself salivate at the thought of white crusty bread spread thickly with butter.

The refectory was deserted when he got there. All the tables were out, ready for breakfast, but the lights were off and the kitchen hatch was closed. There was a side door set next to the hatch. He tried the handle, expecting it to be locked. But it gave. The kitchen was lit by the blue light of a fly-zapper. It shone off the silver work surfaces like moonlight.

There was no food left out anywhere. He opened a door; it led into a larder, but there were just bags of dried food in there – rice and flour. Nothing he could just eat.

A huge fridge stood at the back of the room. He walked past preparation stations, rows of saucepans big enough to bath a baby in, plastic chopping boards in shades of grey that must have been red or blue or green in proper light. He reached the fridge and tugged the handle. Locked.

If this were Northdene, he could just find the boy in charge of the tuck shop and pay double the daytime price for a Mars bar.

But this wasn't Northdene.

And there was nothing to eat.

Suddenly, the back door opened. The dinner lady walked in. Curtis thought about ducking under a table, but there wasn't time, and anyway the space under the nearest table was crammed with oven trays and cake tins.

She put down the shopping bag she was carrying and raised one eyebrow.

'Hello,' Curtis said.

'Hello,' she said doubtfully. 'What are you doing in here? And if you say Midnight Feast you'll be sorry. This isn't Enid Blyton, you know.'

'I know. I just . . . I missed dinner.'

'Why?'

'I fell asleep. I didn't mean to, it just happened.'

'Why did no one wake you?'

'I don't think anyone noticed I was missing.'

There was silence. The woman unbuttoned her jacket and folded it on top of her shopping bag. 'I've finished work. I haven't got time to switch everything on again and cook a meal.'

'I know. I didn't expect you to. Why would you?' Curtis's stomach rumbled so loudly they could both hear it.

The corner of the woman's mouth rose. 'But it just so happens that sometimes, before I go to bed, I make myself a hot chocolate and some toast with jam. You could share, if you want.'

Curtis nodded, then remembered his manners. 'Yes, please.'

She flicked some of the light switches next to the door and unlocked the fridge.

Soon, Curtis was sitting in a plastic chair, pulled up to the main prep table, with a cup of hot chocolate and thick toast smeared with red jam.

'Don't make a habit of this, will you?' the dinner lady said, taking a bite of her own toast. 'I don't cook all that food for you lot to leave it to go to waste.'

Curtis shook his head. The hum of the fridge and the crunch of the crusts were the only noises.

'I'm Curtis,' he said, after he'd licked the jam off his fingers.

'Pleased to meet you. I'm Mrs Shanklin. You can call me Carol.'

'Thank you for the toast, Carol.'

'You're welcome. Things don't seem so bad do they, on a full stomach?' She smiled at him.

Curtis felt his cheeks get hot. 'Did I look like things seemed bad?'

'You had that air about you, yes. I'm guessing you're homesick? It happens a lot. First time away from home, is it?'

Curtis frowned. 'No, the exact opposite, really.'

'Oh?'

'I was at Northdene Prep. I was a boarder. So, I'm used to being away from home. But . . . I had to leave.'

Carol took a sip of her chocolate. 'Why?'

Curtis looked at the crumbs on his plate. He licked the tip of his index finger and dabbed them up. 'Money,' he said finally. 'I needed a scholarship. If you're clever enough, then they let you go there for free. I sat the exam.' Curtis paused. He put his head in his hands.

'Are you OK?'

He nodded quickly. 'I didn't pass.'

'Life's full of surprises,' Carol said. 'Things that you think are one way turn out to be another. But things have a way of working out in the end. I've been here all my life. I didn't expect that when I started here. I was sure I'd be an actress or a singer. But I don't regret it. I'm happy here. You might be too if you give it a chance.' She took his plate and balanced it on top of hers; she carried them to the sink and ran the hot water.

'I can do that,' Curtis said. He took her place at the sink and added washing-up liquid. 'You like it here?'

Carol laughed. 'It has its moments.'

'Some people think the house is haunted.'

Carol picked up a plate from the draining board and wiped it with a tea towel. She chuckled. 'The Wickworth Boy? Have you been talking to Year 7s?'

'You've heard of him?'

'Of course. Poor thing. My gran used to work here when she was a girl. She saw him once, wandering the upper house. He walked right past her. She said she was rooted to the spot with fear. She heard him calling too, one night, calling for his mother.'

'His mother? I thought he lost his true love?'

Carol took the cloth from him and wiped the draining board. 'Is that what they say now? The maids used to say it was his mother he'd lost. But then, those maids went to live in the big house when they were just girls. They probably thought everyone was missing their mother.'

Curtis thought of his phone upstairs. The one that hadn't rung the whole time he'd been at Wickworth. 'I should go now,' he said.

Carol nodded. Then she suddenly looked serious. 'And you should try to get to know a few people here. They're not bad kids, you know. You need someone to wake you up if you sleep through tea time again.'

The house beyond the kitchen was in darkness. The moon had risen and silver light fell in through the windows, striping the ground like the keys on a piano. He thought about what Carol had said, about having people to watch out for him. She was right.

Would Paige be asleep? Was it too late to apologise? He walked towards Bluebell to see.

As he got closer, he heard Paige's voice coming from inside. 'No, he wasn't at tea, I told you.'

The door to her room was slightly ajar. Curtis stood in the corridor. Were they talking about him?

'Well, where is he then?' Jo asked.

'Why do you care? I thought you were meant to be *my* friend.'

'I am your friend. Don't be daft. I just wondered that's all. I think he's kind of cute, don't you?'

'Cute?' Paige sounded horrified.

'Yes. Not as cute as Liam, though.'

Curtis heard Paige squeal in disgust. 'Joanne Cartwright, you are one strange girl.'

'I feel a bit sorry for him.' Sal's voice was soft. 'He doesn't know anyone. And he's kind of awkward. As though he doesn't know what to say.'

Curtis felt his stomach turn cold. He reached out and leaned against the corridor wall. Sal felt sorry for him. Sal, who crept around like a mouse doing whatever Paige and Jo told her to do. He couldn't believe it.

He breathed in and out, slowly.

'He's always got something to say,' Paige said. 'Some la-di-da nonsense every time he opens his mouth. You should have heard him today, "There's a scientific explanation for everything."' She spoke in a plummy voice, a cross between Hugh Grant and Prince William; *nothing* like the way he spoke. "'The world is round,'" she continued, "'and so is my massive head. I know everything about everything. And you are an idiot.'"

Jo burst out laughing. 'Do it again!'

"'My name is Curtis Maximilian Frederick Okafor and I am a Northdene Prep boy. Ask me any question and my computer-brain will uncover the answer in seconds. There is nothing I don't know.'"

'Can I ask a question?' Jo asked.

"'Fire away, old chum.'"

'What is the square root of six hundred and forty-five?'

'No,' Paige said in her real voice. 'No maths. Ask me something else.'

'Oh, OK. Well, why are you here and not at Northdene any more?'

"'Righto. Well, I had to leave, you see. I accidentally burned down the science lab. I was attempting to prove that fire is hot. So I lit a match too close to a Bunsen burner and – whoosh – the place was burned to a crisp in moments. After that, the dear headmaster asked me not to come back. So I'm slumming it with chavs, old bean.'"

There were howls of laughter coming from inside Bluebell now. Curtis pressed his eyes closed, ignoring the sting of tears. But he couldn't close his ears. Paige was whooping and gasping for air.

Curtis took two steps closer to the door. He should go in. He should go in and confront them; he should yell and tell them that they had him all wrong, that he wasn't like that at all.

But he didn't go in.

He couldn't walk into the middle of their laughter.

Curtis turned away.

He didn't care what they thought. He wasn't their friend, anyway. He didn't even like Paige. There was no way he was going to apologise to her now.

He didn't need anyone. Carol was wrong. He was better off by himself.

CHAPTER 17

Paige's sides ached from laughing. She had tipped off the bed on to the floor and now lay there, still giggling. 'This is good, isn't it? Fun, I mean.' She looked across at Sal on the bottom bunk, then Jo above her. 'It's nice being here, having a laugh. I think I'm going to like senior school.'

Jo nodded. 'Me too. We're meeting some nice people in our group, aren't we, Sal?'

'Hmm,' Sal agreed slowly. 'I suppose.'

'No one as nice as me, I hope,' Paige said. 'You're still my best mates.'

'Of course we are,' Jo said. 'I'm just saying.'

Paige felt a sudden stab of unease. It had always been the three of them. Was this the change that the tarot cards had seen? Was that what The Tower had meant on the first day? She picked up her washbag. 'I'm going to clean my teeth,' she said. 'Either of you coming?'

'I did mine before,' Sal said.

Jo pulled her duvet up to her chin. 'Nope. Part of the fun of being on holiday is that you don't have to clean your teeth. Anyway, it's gone lights-out. You'll be in trouble if Mrs Burton-Jones catches you again.'

'Fine. I'll go by myself.' Paige headed out to the bathroom. It was one floor down, on the landing below. The lights were off, though there was a green glow from the fire exit sign. She kept one hand on the wall, to help find her way. She stepped soundlessly in her slippers: down the stairs, along the corridor, as far as the bathroom. She pushed open the heavy door. There was no one left inside, but the mirrors were still misted up from the people earlier. It felt warm and damp, like a rainforest. There were a row of mirrors, some sinks, four toilet cubicles and three showers, one of them drip-drip-dripping water into its tray.

Paige propped her washbag on the edge of a sink and wiped a clear patch in the mist on the mirror. She hummed quietly to herself as she cleaned her teeth.

It had been a weird day. Laughing with Jo and Sal had been fun, but then hearing about their new friends made her brain feel itchy. Her arms were starting to ache from the climbing. And then there was that horrible feeling of being pushed off the rock. There had *definitely* been something there, beside her, while she climbed.

She spat into the sink and swilled some water around her mouth.

The pipes grumbled and knocked as water ran through them.

She turned off the tap.

The pipes kept on knocking.

Knock.

Knock.

Knock.

Paige thumped the tap. Stupid old house. She looked at the mirror again. It had misted over. All she could see was her own vague, pink and yellow shape reflected back at her. She wiped it again with a squeak. A drop of water rolled down the glass.

What was that?

Had something moved behind her?

She spun around.

The room was empty.

But the noise from the pipes continued, like a faraway drum getting closer. Or like the rattle of coach wheels on a stony road.

'Is something there?' Paige whispered. 'Show yourself!'

There was a whispering sound. Wind through trees? Or something else?

She turned back to the mirror slowly. Mum said that mirrors could be routes into other worlds. She said that at Halloween if you spoke the name of a dead person three times in front of a mirror, then you would dream about them that night.

Paige took a deep breath. It wasn't Halloween, but it might work anyway. Did she dare?

'Wickworth Boy,' she whispered.

The knocks got louder, matching the insistent thumping in her chest.

'Wickworth Boy,' she said.

'Wickworth Boy.'

Silence.

The thumping stopped. Paige held her breath. She looked at the mirror. The mist had cleared. Her own face looked back, green eyes wide with fear.

Paige picked up her washbag and clenched it to her chest.

Why had she done that?

Stupid, stupid.

She backed away from the mirror, keeping an eye on it the whole time.

She yanked the bathroom door and staggered out. The landing was deserted. And then she saw it. A white mist hovered at the far end of the corridor. She stifled a moan. It twisted in the air.

'Paige,' a voice whispered.

'Who is it?' she stammered.

'Paige. We're coming.'

There was a surge of energy, like static electricity bouncing along the walls. Paige felt it hit her and all the hairs on her arms rose. Her heart leapt in her chest.

She dropped her washbag.

And ran.

The sound of ghostly laughter floated up the stairs behind her.

Paige's heart was hammering like hooves at a gallop. She felt sick. This was real. She had believed it was before, but now she knew. She knew in the same way that she knew which way was up or that the sun would rise tomorrow. The Wickworth Boy was real and he was looking for her. They had messed with something big. Spirits were on the move.

She lay on her bed with her eyes open. She stared at the ceiling just half a metre or so from her face. Sal and Jo were breathing gently, fast asleep.

The Wickworth Boy had come for her.

And she had been so scared.

Paige felt her face get hot.

If anyone had asked her whether she was brave or not, a few days ago she would have said yes, definitely, no question.

Now she wasn't so sure.

She rubbed her cheeks. If Mum had seen a ghost, she would have talked to it, not run away. She would have asked what it wanted and how she could help. Mum said that ghosts were just people who weren't ready to say goodbye.

If only she could call Mum. But she couldn't. Mum believed phones only rang at night if it was bad news. Paige couldn't frighten Mum like that.

In the dark, a different idea began to form. She couldn't call home for advice, but she could do the next best thing. She had her tarot pack with her. She could try to find out what the Wickworth Boy wanted. She could be brave.

She climbed down out of her bunk quietly, then riffled in her bag until her fingers wrapped around the pack.

Where could she do it?

It was too dark in here and if she switched on a light, it would wake the others. For some reason, she didn't want to tell them what she'd seen. Not yet, anyway.

The painting.

She should do it in front of the painting. Curtis wouldn't mind being woken up. And she didn't care if he did mind. He had been horrible to her all day. The painting wasn't his, anyway. It wasn't his property.

Paige put on her dressing gown and slippers and left Bluebell. She walked quickly along the corridor. Outside his room, she paused and then knocked gently.

She heard a noise from inside.

Was it 'come in'? It was close enough. She pushed open the door. Her eyes took a minute to adjust to the darkness. She could make out a lump on the bed; it turned over, then sat up. 'Paige?' Curtis said. His voice sounded thick, as if he had a cold. 'What do you want? Leave me alone.'

'It isn't you I'm here for. It's the Boy.' Paige avoided the piles of junk in the room and walked over to the window. She pulled open the curtain. The sky outside twinkled with stars. The moon was as round as a saucer of milk. It was clear and bright enough to see the lawn and the lake below.

'What are you doing?' Curtis said. 'What do you want?'

Paige ignored him. She glanced around the room for the painting. It was propped against the end of the bed. She swivelled it slightly so that it was in a better position.

'Hey,' Curtis said, sitting up.

'It isn't yours. I need it for a minute.' She sat down in front of it and took out her cards. She shuffled them quickly. Then she laid the pack between her and the painting and cut the deck once, then twice.

Curtis leaned over the edge of the bed to watch her. He didn't say anything. Paige concentrated on the pack, ignoring the sound of Curtis's snuffly breathing. She turned over the cards and arranged them in a cross shape: the Page of Swords, the Empress, the Nine of Swords, the Knight of Cups, the Sun, the Four of Pentacles, the World.

Two sets of dark eyes watched her in the moonlight, one static, oil on canvas, the other curious, alert.

'What are you doing?'

'I thought you didn't believe in it.'

'I don't. I just wondered, that's all.'

Paige wasn't exactly sure what all the cards meant in the positions she'd put them. But Mum always insisted that didn't matter, what was important was to try to see what message the cards were giving.

'Worry,' she said finally. 'Disappointment.' Her fingers rested on the Page of Swords. 'This one means an angry boy. The Empress might be a mother, or some other woman. You see the World here, between them? The boy travelled away from the woman. This card,' she pointed to the Knight of Cups, 'this is a letter or a phone call.'

Curtis snorted. 'A phone call. In 1805?'

'Yes, OK. Maybe not a phone call. A letter then. And I can see hard work and disappointment here too,' Paige said.

'What about that one then?' Curtis pointed to the laughing, carefree face of the Sun. 'That isn't disappointment.'

'No,' Paige snapped. 'It isn't. That one's usually a good card. Why don't you leave me alone to get on with this?'

The mattress creaked as Curtis settled down on it. 'You're the one who came barging in here in the middle of the night.'

Curtis was finally silent. Paige looked at the spread of cards in front of her. Her eyes kept flicking back to the Empress; a woman with long robes and a crown sitting on a throne surrounded by trees. This card was the heart of it, she was sure. This is what the Boy was searching for. Was it his mother? His girlfriend? Paige frowned in concentration. 'He's angry that he had to leave her. Frightened too, maybe,' she said softly.

There was a silence.

Then, Curtis spoke. He was so quiet that she could hardly hear him. 'The trouble with that stuff. Astrology and things. Is that you can read anything you like into it. The way you said it, it could have been me you were talking about.'

'You?' Paige looked up at him.

'Me, or you, or anyone. You could make it fit anyone's life. Who hasn't been angry or disappointed?'

'What's a posh boy like you got to be disappointed about?'

Curtis twisted around on the bed so that he faced her. Paige was surprised by how angry he looked. His eyes were screwed up tight. 'What do you know about me? Hey? You don't know anything.'

Paige leaned away from him; a flicker of anxiety stirred in her belly.

'I heard you before. I *heard* you,' he said.

'What?' Paige asked. 'What are you talking about?'

'I heard you. I heard you laughing about me with Sal and Jo. You did a stupid impression of me that wasn't even accurate. I was outside your door. I *heard* you.'

Paige tried to remember what she'd said. Something about Bunsen burners? She shrugged. 'It was just a joke. We were just having a laugh.'

'Yes. Hysterical.' The last word was almost spat out.

'I didn't mean to be nasty. I'm not a nasty person.'

'No, you're just thoughtless.'

Was she? Was that how he saw her? Paige looked down at the cards. Mum always said she had good intuition. That she saw things that other people didn't. She wasn't thoughtless. She was sure she wasn't. 'I'm not,' she said quietly.

'You haven't even tried to get to know me. You've just made assumptions the way everyone else has.'

'Well, so have you! You've been avoiding me. And you've laughed at the things I believe. You haven't given me a chance either!' Paige sat up, leaning towards him.

They stared at each other, eyes locked in anger. Between them, the painting of the Boy gleamed in the moonlight.

'Well, that's because you're mental,' he snapped.

'No, you're mental.'

'No, you are.'

'You are.'

Curtis made a noise that Paige thought at first was a laugh. Then she realised it was more like a sob. Curtis covered his face with his hands. Had she gone too far? She couldn't think of anything to say so she put her hand on his arm and left it there. He didn't move away. Slowly, he wiped his face with the back of his sleeve and managed a small smile.

'Do you think this is how brothers and sisters behave?' he asked.

'I dunno. It's just me at home.'

'Me too.'

Was he lonely, maybe? 'What did you mean before,' she asked, 'when you said that the cards could have been talking about you?'

CHAPTER 18

Curtis frowned. Paige was looking up at him; her hair was silver in the moonlight and her eyes were wide with concern. She really wanted to know. And, he found, to his surprise, that he really wanted to tell her. He took a deep breath.

'I went to Northdene when I was six. My parents thought I'd have the best start in life there. And I did, it was a brilliant school. But then, well, Mum lost her job last year. She earned more than Dad. There wasn't enough money to keep me there.'

'So you had to leave?' Paige asked.

'No, not straight away. There was one chance and it was down to me. I could take the exam to become a scholarship boy. That means you go for free, if you're clever enough.' Curtis paused. His palms felt cold and damp, despite the heat of the room. 'It was my one opportunity. I messed it up. I knew the answers, I did. But when I sat down in the exam room, I . . . I sort of lost it. Like a breakdown, really. Nothing came out the way I meant. I failed. And it was all my fault.'

He felt again the panic and desperation of being in that room; the feeling that the walls were creeping closer, the ceiling dropping down, pinning him and crushing him. He hadn't been able to move, had barely been able to breathe. The words on the exam paper had made no sense and his answers, when he finally wrote them down, had made even less.

'Couldn't you take the exam again?'

He shook his head. 'I'd only fail again. I know I would. You know, my mum hasn't been able to look me in the eye all summer. She's too ashamed.'

'No way.'

'What?'

'I don't reckon your mum's ashamed. She wanted what was best for you, didn't she? She didn't send you to that school so that she could show off to her mates that she was rolling in money. She did it for you. She probably feels like she's the one who's let you down. She lost her job, didn't she? My mum always goes into a strop when we can't afford things. It doesn't mean she's cross with me.'

Paige tidied away the pack of cards. Instead of

putting the last one in the box, she passed it to Curtis. The Empress.

'Maybe this is for you,' she said. 'Maybe it *was* your reading. I don't even know if you can do a reading for a portrait, Mum never said.'

The card felt waxy in his hand. 'Thanks,' he said. He wasn't sure what he was meant to do with it. There was just enough light to make out the Empress's face. She was smiling. It was a benign smile, as though she was giving a blessing to someone just out of view.

'The phone call!' Paige said.

'What?'

'I saw a phone call in the spread. You should ring your mum!'

Curtis felt his heart thud faster. 'It's late.'

'Does she have a phobia of late-night phone calls?'

'What? No, of course not.'

'So there's no reason not to phone her. I bet she'd love to hear from you. When was the last time you talked to her properly?'

Curtis shrugged. The last time he could remember feeling that things might be OK was when Mum found out that the scholarship exam existed. She had been distant and irritable for months but when she'd told him that he could take the exam she'd hugged him tight and it had seemed, for a moment, that everything would be OK.

And then he'd failed.

'Where's your phone?' Paige was up off the floor and opening his case.

'Leave that. I've got it here.' Curtis fished around on the bed until he found it. Was he really going to do this?

'Well, go on. Dial the number.'

Curtis tapped a few icons. Then he could hear it ringing. Mum's phone would be next to her bed. Would it wake her up? Would she be cross?

'Hello?' a sleepy voice answered.

'Mum?'

'Curtis, is that you? Is everything OK? What time is it?'

His mouth suddenly felt dry.

'Curtis?'

'Yes, it's me, Mum. I was just calling to, well . . . I just thought I'd call, that's all.'

'Are you OK? Is there a problem?' Mum said.

'No, no problem.' There was a silence. Curtis felt his eyes prickle. This was just making it worse. He shouldn't have rung in the middle of the night. 'Look, Mum. Everything's fine. I'll call again.'

'Curtis?'

'Got to go. Bye.' Curtis ended the call and switched off his phone. He dropped it back down on to the bed.

'Wow. I've heard friendlier chats between brick walls,' Paige said.

Curtis didn't answer.

'You keep the Empress,' Paige said. 'I'll want her back before the end of the week. But you keep her for now. You need her.'

CHAPTER 19

CJTE/019 Notice from Felix Barley's Avon Journal
18th C.

The gossip came first from the footmen. They were
the ones who tidied away the master's newspapers
after morning tea. They had seen the notice. The
footmen told the cook, who told the gardener,
who told the stableman. And so the news passed
throughout the household as far as the coach
boy. A negro slave had run away. Five guineas was
offered for persons securing his return.

The stableman asked if he knew the runaway. He
did not. They might share a skin colour, but they
were strangers. The runaway had lived over fifteen
miles away, a day's journey.

The coach boy cried. Not for the runaway, but
because his mother had been wrong. The rumour in
the dark, treacle heat of the boiling shed had

been wrong. There was a reward for the return of a runaway slave. They were no freer here than they had been at home. The sickening journey had been for nothing. He had left Maggie for nothing.

CHAPTER 20

Curtis opened his eyes. Sunlight hit the bed. The tarot card was propped up close to him. The Empress, smiling. Things always looked better after a night's sleep, he thought. Well, at least they didn't seem any worse. He turned his phone on. Three missed calls, two from Mum, one from Dad. Great. Wanting to shout at him for waking them up in the middle of the night, no doubt.

So much for the Empress watching out for him. He took the card and went downstairs.

It was Art this morning. He'd missed most of it on his first day. Curtis made his way to the converted barn in the courtyard. Paige was there already waiting outside.

She grinned when she saw him. 'Morning.'

Curtis fished the tarot card from his back pocket and handed it to her. 'Hello. You can have this back. Thanks for lending it to me, but I don't need it.'

'You sure?'

'Yes. I'm not planning a career as a warlock any time soon.'

'Hey! Are you teasing me?'

Curtis smiled. 'I think so.'

'Good. That's what friends do.'

'Are we friends?'

'Not yet. But we could be. Don't you think?'

'Maybe.' He smiled a little. How had she become a friend? He hadn't even noticed it happening.

Paige led the way into the classroom. It had changed since that first day. The whole of the central space was filled by an enormous wicker ball. It reached right up to the roof. The sticks were woven in and out of each other in a lattice.

'Wow!' Paige said. 'That's amazing. What is it?'

'A huge wicker ball. How are they going to get it out?'

'Hit it with a giant tennis racquet?'

Everyone else in the group was busy opening drawers and pulling out supplies. They knew exactly what was going on. Paige dived straight in, asking quick questions of the people on either side. Curtis watched her return with two armfuls of tissue paper. She thrust it towards him. 'You'll need this.'

'What are we doing?'

'Making the earth.'

Oh. The wicker was just the skeleton, the earth's crust, waiting for tissue paper continents to be glued on. He wondered for a second whether he could persuade them to make Pangaea, the lost continent, the way things were right at the beginning. Then he sighed. It was going to be hard enough to make the world as it really was without bringing ancient history into it.

'I saw the World last night, do you remember?' Paige shoved his tissue out of the way and dropped scissors and glue on to the table. 'In the cards?'

'Yes.' Curtis reached to get his tissue paper back.

'I thought it might mean something about the Boy travelling. I didn't think it meant this. Do you want to make a bit of the Atlantic with me?'

'He might have travelled. I went to the library yesterday. I didn't have a chance to tell you. I was too busy –'

'Ignoring me?' Paige interrupted.

'Well, yes, I suppose so. Sorry.'

'It's all right. I was ignoring you too. Pass me some blue.'

Curtis pushed the pile of paper back towards her. 'He might have come from the West Indies. Even Africa, maybe. He might have been a slave.'

'Slaves? In Britain? I didn't think there were any here. I thought it was, I dunno, a foreign thing.'

'Yes, there were slaves here. I want to find out if he was one.'

'Were your family slaves? Do you think that's why he's trying to communicate with us?'

Curtis turned to face Paige. She was busy overlapping paper and hadn't noticed that he'd stopped. 'What?' he asked.

'You know. He might see you as a kindred spirit, or something.'

'My mum's parents are from Nigeria.'

'Were they slaves?'

'Of course not. If anything, their family might have been slave traders. Some Nigerians were ages ago.'

'Ooh,' Paige looked up. Her eyes shone. 'So your family might have sold him into slavery. He might be after revenge.'

'You are completely mental, do you know that?' Curtis picked up a piece of tissue paper and started hacking at it with his scissors. 'You're a classic fantasist. You don't let facts get in the way of your vision of the world, do you? I shouldn't be encouraging you. I should get you some professional help.'

'Are you teasing me again?'

'No.'

'Oh.'

Neither of them said anything for a while. Paige clipped carefully; she was making a pattern that reminded Curtis of fish scales. His was more, well, avant garde.

'You're doing it wrong,' Paige said eventually.

'I'm making Art. You're just doing craft.'

'Yours looks a mess.'

'It's meant to. It represents climate chaos, over-fishing, pollution, that sort of thing.'

'You just don't know how to cut tissue paper properly.'

'I do, but I'm choosing not to.'

'Now who's the fantasist? So, how are we going to find out? I mean whether he was a slave or not?'

Curtis put down his scissors. 'I don't know. More research, I suppose. We need to go back to the library.'

'Libraries are boring,' Paige said. 'I've got a much better idea.'

CHAPTER 21

'Libraries aren't boring,' Curtis said. 'The one here is nice.'

'Nice? You're weird, you know that? Listen, after this we've got a break. Then dinner. Then canoeing. I've got an idea we can try at breaktime.'

'Why do I feel worried? Oh yes, because your last brilliant idea saw me standing in Mrs Burton-Jones's room apologising.'

'Don't be like that. This one isn't going to get us into any trouble.'

Curtis picked up their pile of snipped paper and carried it towards the centre of the room, where Mr Appleton was supervising the gluing. Paige followed.

'What's your idea?' he asked.

She grinned. She knew he'd come around. 'Dowsing.'

'What?'

'My mum uses it when she's lost something. What you do is, you take two sticks and you hold them in front of you. Then, when you're close to the thing you're looking for, they cross.'

'Oh, I know. People do it when they're looking for water. Actually, I think there is some kind of scientific basis for that, it's something to do with ions –'

Oh, Curtis was so annoying. Paige sighed dramatically. 'Yes. But it doesn't have to be for water. You can look for anything that way.'

Paige dipped a fat brush into a pot of PVA glue. Instead of painting the tissue paper, she blobbed a bit on the back of her hand. When it dried, she could peel it off like loose skin. Cool.

'And what exactly are we looking for?' Curtis asked, taking the brush from her.

'Hey, I was enjoying that.'

'What do you intend to dowse for?'

She thought about the twisting white mist she'd seen near the bathroom last night. Her face became more serious. 'Well. Ghosts. They want to tell us something. I can feel it. We just have to make sure we're listening. It's all about allowing yourself to be open to the signals.'

'I'm not a mobile phone mast, you know.'

'Actually, if you let yourself be, that's exactly what you are.'

Mr Appleton called for everyone's attention. 'Great work this morning, Year 6. We'll have a splendid creation by the time the week is out. Clear up now. Fifteen minutes' break, then head in for lunch. This afternoon, be sure to put on quick-drying clothes. Canoeing, you know. It gets a bit damp.'

Paige grabbed a couple of lengths of spare willow while Curtis cleared their area. 'Come on,' she said. 'This will be fun.'

Paige took Curtis out to the lawn in front of the house. Another group were out here. They sat in the shade of the trees. The lake looked inviting, cool against the heat of the midday sun. But there was no time for swimming.

'We'll start here,' Paige said.

'But there's loads of people about,' Curtis answered.

'It's true. They might disrupt the signals. But we've only got fifteen minutes.'

Curtis frowned.

Paige gave him a light punch on the arm. She knew he hadn't really been worried about the others being signal disrupters. He was more worried about looking like an idiot. But that was never anything to worry about. 'Ready?'

Curtis shoved his hands into his pockets, but nodded.

Paige held out the sticks in front of her and concentrated hard on the Wickworth Boy. She tried to see his face in her mind; his dark hair, skin the colour of bark and eyes that were angry and sad and kind, all at once.

As soon as she could see him clearly, she took a few steps forward. The grass was springy under her feet. She breathed gently. The sounds around her faded. It was just her and the dowsing rods that mattered.

'Have you found anything yet?' Curtis asked.

Paige sighed. 'No. This could take a while. Why don't you get two sticks and help me?'

'I don't know how to do it.'

'It doesn't matter. It's a gift. Either you can do it, or you can't. Simple as that. Go and get some sticks and let me concentrate.'

Curtis edged away slowly. She wasn't sure that he would join in, but at least he wasn't staring at her the whole time now either.

She took another slow breath and felt the delicate weight of the wicker in her hands. They were still, but as soon as she was on the trail, she knew they would leap and bounce, crossing and uncrossing like windscreen wipers on the blink. It was how she and Mum found the car keys quite often.

She imagined the boy in the painting smiling, beckoning her on. She took a few slow steps. Towards the lake. One of the rods turned gently, like a weather vane changing direction. She moved closer to the water. The other rod rotated too. They were both swaying together: left, pause, right, pause. They were picking up an energy, though it was still weak.

As she stepped on to the wooden jetty that stuck out over the lake, she felt one of the rods kick and leap in her hands.

The hairs on the back of her neck raised as though a spectral mouth had blown on them. She was close to something, she could feel it.

She stepped back on to dry land. The rods settled back into their gentle spin.

Forward on to the jetty. The rods twitched and crossed like a beginner's baton class.

It was the jetty. Something was here, on the jetty.

Paige walked further out. On either side red and blue canoes bumped in the breeze. Soon, the rods in her hands were moving so fast they were scratching her palms; the air seemed dense and cold against her skin, despite the sunlight. Her heartbeat quickened. Something had happened here. The ghost of it lingered, like the sour feeling in a room after a row. She could feel the Wickworth Boy, trying to push his way through. Pressing down on her. Crushing her.

'Gotcha!'

Paige squealed as a hand clamped down on her shoulder. 'Curtis! You scared the life out of me!'

'Sorry. You just looked like you were off in your own little world. I couldn't resist.'

'Well, try.'

'OK. Sorry. Have you found something?'

'I think so. Here, do you want a go?' She handed the sticks to Curtis. He raised a suspicious eyebrow.

'If you don't take it seriously, then the spirits won't work for you,' she said.

Curtis shrugged. 'The way I see it, my own subconscious is creating tiny electrical impulses in my nerves. Whenever my unconscious mind sees something it wants me to pay attention to, it will fire off the nerve endings. So, if this doesn't work, then I've no one to blame but myself. What do I have to do?'

Paige moved beside Curtis and held his wrists. 'Hold them like this, loose, but firm. OK? Then picture what you want to find in your mind. Try and see it really clearly. Then look for it. You'll know when the rods have found something.'

Curtis nodded, but he was grinning like a cat in an ice cream van. He wasn't taking this seriously at all.

Paige felt a sudden shiver of alarm. Should she really let him do this, if he wasn't going to be respectful? What if the ghosts got angry?

'Don't worry,' Curtis said. 'Nothing bad can happen. I'm not running with scissors here.'

Paige gave a swift nod. 'I think there's something on the jetty. Walk on the grass and concentrate, just to get a feel for it. The sticks went crazy a second ago.'

She watched Curtis. Would he feel the same presence as she had?

He circled on the lawn for a few minutes, then turned towards her. He was still grinning. She frowned – if the ghosts didn't get angry, she might. 'Wipe that smirk off your face and concentrate,' she said.

He forced his mouth into a frown, but Paige could tell there were giggles just below the surface.

Until he stepped on to the jetty.

'What on earth?' he said. The rods had leapt in his hands. 'I didn't do that!' he said. She could hear a ripple of panic in his voice.

'Of course not,' Paige answered.

'I mean it. That wasn't me, or my subconscious. But it *had* to be. What else could it be? It was because you planted the suggestion. You Derren Browned me. You put the idea in my head.'

'I did not,' Paige said hotly. 'You're dowsing. That's what happens. What we need to work out is, why here? What happened here?'

Paige watched Curtis pace backwards and forwards a few times. Each time he stepped on to the wooden jetty, the dowsing rods moved. He stopped. 'What?' Paige asked.

'I think it's all the ions in the water. Dowsing is meant to find water, after all. I think all it's telling us is that there's a lake here. I'm going to walk around a bit more and see what happens. Without you suggesting anything.'

'Fine. We need more info anyway. And I won't say a thing. My lips are sealed. Nothing but silence.'

'Well, shh then.'

Curtis circled out over the lawn, moving towards the house.

Paige gave one last look at the lake. Tiny, choppy waves lapped at the canoes; ripples spread in circles where fish broke through to the surface. What had happened here? Was this where the Boy and his love met?

'Hey, Paige,' Curtis shouted.

He stood at the side of the house. Even from this distance, she could make out the movement of the dowsing sticks. She ran over to him.

'I think, I'm not sure, but I think, they want me to go this way. They twitch when I point at the house.'

'Well, follow them then!' Paige said.

110

He led the way. Each careful step he took, he would pause and wait for a response from the rods.

Paige had to bite her tongue, to stop herself telling him to get a move on.

He moved around the side of the house, past the kitchen door. They were back in the courtyard. A group of children with their faces painted blue and green clattered past them. Sal was one of them. Paige caught her eye and raised an eyebrow.

'Ancient Celts,' Sal said and shrugged.

'Oh,' Paige said. Made perfect sense. She gave a little wave and hurried up after Curtis. He crossed the cobbled yard and stood in front of the Art Barn.

'My subconscious wants us to go in there,' he said.

The barn was empty. Somehow, without the movement and sound of people around it, the wicker globe looked even bigger. Some of it was covered in green and blue tissue and coloured light fell through like stained glass. The room was warm and smelled of glue and paper dust.

Curtis looked down at his hands. The sticks were crossing rapidly like chopsticks in a Chinese restaurant.

'Amazing, isn't it?' she asked.

'It's an amazing phenomenon; the motive power of auto-suggestion.'

'What?'

'It means my mind can make stuff move. There's a perfectly rational explanation.'

'Then why do you look so worried?' It was true. There was a tremor in his voice as though he was a tiny bit scared of what he was seeing.

'I'm not worried. I'm simply fascinated by my brain's ability to dupe my body. It isn't worry.'

'Well, it's doing a very good impression.'

Curtis rolled his eyes.

'Where does it want you to go?' Paige asked, leaning in to look at his hands.

'I don't know. How can I tell?'

Paige looked at him. There was no sarcasm now, just interest and a tiny touch of fear. She smiled. 'It's OK. Just let your mind clear. Don't try too hard. All he needs is for you to listen. He'll tell you where to go.'

Curtis stepped into the centre of the room, then veered right. He followed a side wall. There was a small flight of steps, more like a ladder, really, tucked into the far corner. It was made of slats of wood, worn in the centre by hundreds of years' worth of footsteps. A handrail ran up against the stone wall, but there were no railings or banister on the other side.

'Here?' Paige whispered.

'I guess so.'

Curtis led the way, holding the dowsing rods in front of him and using his elbow against the wall to keep his balance. Paige gripped the handrail. The steps creaked as they climbed.

They were just below a wide ledge.

Miles above the main room.

Paige stopped.

'What is it?' Curtis asked.

'Nothing.' Her heartbeat quickened and her knees felt as though they were filling up with jelly. 'But I'm not coming any further.'

The ledge was wider than a shelf, but not by much. And there was nothing along the edge to stop a person from falling and cracking their head open on the floor below. Paige pressed her shoulder blades against the wall. The solid stone against her back made her feel a bit calmer. But there was no way she was going any higher.

'Is there anything up there?' she asked. Her voice sounded squeaky, like a mouse with its tail trapped in a door.

Curtis moved on to the ledge and poked around. It creaked under his weight.

Paige took a deep breath and tried not to think about the drop. From where she stood, she could just make out a few cardboard boxes and a sack made of some brown rough-looking stuff.

'I don't think so. I can't see anything interesting.'
Paige heard rustling as he moved some things around.
'No, nothing. It's just art supplies.' Curtis appeared at
the top of the steps. 'I can't see anyth—' He paused. He
was looking out at the room below. His eyes scanned
the walls and the roof, then the walls again.

'What?'

'This room. Look.' He pointed. 'There are marks
where walls used to be. This room wasn't always one
big space.'

Paige looked. She could see what he meant. There
were lines of brick running vertically along the main
wall about three metres apart. It looked as though once
upon a time there had been lots of small walls breaking
up the main space. But she wasn't sure why the Boy
would want them to look at rows of bricks. 'So what?'
she asked.

'Look how far apart the walls were. I bet that if we
looked at an old plan of this place we'd see that the Art
Barn used to be a stables. The portrait shows him in
livery. This is where the coach boy worked. This room
is where he lived.'

Paige gasped. She could see it now, the ghost of the
stables that were so long gone. She could smell the tang
of horses and hear hooves on earth. The light seemed
to dim and the whisper of straw grew in her ears to a

roar. Paige felt her back scrape down the wall, grazing her spine.

'Paige? Are you all right?' Curtis was beside her.

'I . . . I feel funny.'

'Was it the height again?'

Paige felt his arms lifting her up. She was half walked, half carried back to the ground. He dropped her in a chair. She let her head fall down to her knees and breathed slowly until the sick feeling in her stomach passed. 'Curtis,' she whispered. 'We're close to something. I can feel it. Get the dowsing rods, quickly.'

'But, you're not well, we should –'

'Quickly. It's important.'

She sensed rather than saw him go back up the stairs and snatch up the sticks he'd dropped. Then he was back at her side.

'Do you want to do it?' he asked doubtfully.

'No. There's something here with us, right now. It's all around us. You can do it. The Boy is here.'

The skin on her arms tingled. There was an energy in the room that was almost scalding her. The air was charged with it; the particles of dust danced like moving crystals. 'Do it now!' she said.

Curtis swam before her eyes. She had a horrible feeling that she might faint. She focused on his hands, pulling them into view. He gripped the sticks tightly, his knuckles looked almost grey. He thrust them out in front of him and waited. For a second they were still, then they twitched. They flipped and flailed in his hands as though they were alive. They *were* alive in a way, channelling a life that had been and was lost.

Curtis cried out, in surprise and shock. He was wrenched forwards, his arms lunged out as though he was holding a sword.

There was an awful tearing sound.

The sticks in Curtis's hands had pierced through the thin film of tissue glued to the wicker frame. Two small rips, like eyeholes in a mask, cut through the ocean.

Curtis stepped back. The sticks clattered to the ground. 'I didn't mean to do that. Why would I do that?'

'It isn't you, it's the Wickworth Boy. He wanted you to do that. He's trying to tell us something.'

'But it *was* me, wasn't it? I was the one holding the sticks. And look what I did! Look at it! I've ruined it.'

Paige stood up and stepped over. Her head felt clearer now. 'It isn't ruined. It will glue back,' she said softly. 'We have to think about what this means.'

'No!' Curtis stepped away from her. 'This has gone far enough. I'm not doing this your way any more. I found out more in twenty minutes in the library than I did in days of *this*.' He waved at the sticks on the floor.

'Whatever happened here, it was just suggestion and wishful thinking and you seeing things that are just not there.' He turned to leave. 'If you want me, I will be doing *proper* research.' Then he was gone.

CHAPTER 22

The library would be the best place to go. Curtis rubbed his hands on his jeans, desperate to get rid of the impression of the sticks. But the horrible, twitching sensation remained, like holding invisible fish. He stalked across the courtyard towards the house. He passed the kitchen door. It smelled like lasagne. Food. Maybe he needed food. It might calm him down a bit. He nipped through into the refectory.

'Hello, Carol,' he said. 'Could I have something to take away, please? It's a low blood sugar emergency.'

Carol raised an eyebrow. 'Does this look like McDonalds? I thought you were going to get to know some people. You shouldn't scuttle off like this.'

'I'm not scuttling, I promise. And I've kind of made a friend. But I need to do something important and I won't have time after lunch.'

Carol sighed. She handed him some bread and cheese and an apple. 'Will that do? What is it that's so important?'

'1805,' Curtis said. 'Something happened here that I need to find out about. You don't know anything about that year?'

Carol chuckled. 'A bit before my time, love. Before my gran's time, even. What happened then?'

Curtis slipped the apple into his pocket and folded the bread around the cheese. 'The people who lived here died. Patience and William Burton.'

'Oh.' Carol flashed a glance over his shoulder, checking the rows of tables filling with pupils and teachers. 'Good. Mrs Burton-Jones isn't here yet. She doesn't like people nosing about the place, you know. She's a very private person. A bit sensitive about having to let strangers into the old place. To be honest, if the heating bills here weren't so astronomical, there's no way she'd let you lot over the threshold.'

'Does that mean you do know something about Patience and William?' Curtis leaned in close.

'Not much. But I do know that it was considered a real tragedy. Patience died first, then her father. The place went to the elder sister after that. She was a bitter, miserable old thing. When she died it went to her cousin. That's who my gran worked for. There were parties here all the time after that. Gran told me about some of the things those young gents got up to . . . well . . . never mind.'

'Is there anywhere I could look, if I wanted to find out more about Patience?'

Carol picked up a cloth and started wiping down the surface. 'I don't know, love. When they turned this place into an activity centre lots of the old stuff got packed away. I've no idea where it would be. Shoved in a box in an attic, I shouldn't wonder.'

A shock wave ran right down through Curtis from the top of his head to the soles of his feet. A box in an attic!

'Thanks, Carol,' he said. He turned and rushed out of the hall, to the main staircase, then he pounded up as fast as he could run. Right to the top of the house, to his room: an attic filled with boxes.

He dashed open the curtains, showering the room with dust. Then he pulled the lids off cardboard archive boxes and tugged open filing cabinets. Everything was stuffed full of paper; yellowing reams of typed A4; old-fashioned printouts with perforated edges; sepia photographs of long-dead people. There was no order to any of it. He pulled out a few pieces of paper from one of the boxes and glanced at them: an architect's drawing from 1981; a list of players in the village cricket eleven from 1948; a bill for groceries delivered in 1912.

He sat down in the middle of the floor and tugged the nearest box closer.

The painting, resting against the bed frame where Paige had left it last night, now had a thin layer of dust on it.

He bit into his cheese sandwich and started pulling paper out, one sheet at a time. He chewed slowly, laying out patches and snippets of the house's history on the floor. The box was two-thirds empty when he saw something that made him gasp.

It was a photograph.

A photograph of the Boy.

How was that possible?

He tugged it free of the receipts and lists and held it up to the light. It was a black and white photograph, but instead of the boy's skin being dark, it gleamed white. And it was just his face, no neck, no body. But every eyelash, every crease of skin, the purse of his lips, the flare of his nose, every single detail was perfect. It wasn't a photograph of the painting, though the face was identical. This was something else altogether. He flipped the photo over. Written on the back in curling handwriting were the words: *Death mask of a negro boy,*

*provenance unknown, donated to the Fitzgerald Archive
Nov 1953.*

Death mask?

Curtis felt his skin crawl.

He had seen death masks before during a museum visit at Northdene. People had taken wax impressions from the faces of dead bodies and made plaster casts of them. It was gross. Bizarre. And that's what had happened to their Boy. He had been laid out on a slab, washed and then covered in wax.

Curtis felt a wave of nausea hit him.

A *death* mask?

The Boy looked the same age in the death mask and the painting. How old had he been when he died? Curtis pressed his eyes closed, but he could still see an image of the Boy, laid out in his room above the stables. That's where they would have taken him, wouldn't they? His body heavy and lifeless, its heat fading away. And instead of leaving him be, they had poured hot wax on his face, moulding a mask.

The sudden anger that Curtis felt was so strong that he cried out. How could anyone do that to a boy? Why had they done it?

What were the Burtons up to here all those years ago?

He paused, holding the photo.

There was one of them here still. Mrs Burton-Jones. It was her family that had done this. Her precious ancestors. He put the photograph in his pocket and stood up. He wanted answers.

CHAPTER 23

CJTE/044 - Tracts in support of the trade, 18th C.

The hue and cry following the loss of the
runaway had settled. There had been no sign of
the boy, who was no doubt lost in the throngs
of London. But now curiosity followed the coach
boy wherever he went. Though he rode atop the
coach on outings and jaunts, just as ever, the
looks he received had changed. Especially in the
city. When the coach rattled over the cobblestones
of the quay and the seabirds searched through
the middens, the stevedores kept a watchful eye
on him. Some, those who listened to the speakers
in the Quaker meeting house or read tracts by
Wilberforce, wished him liberty. Others, who
listened to the merchants and read their words,
saw their own ruin in his freedom. But none
ignored him.

The boy, sitting next to the coachman, felt every eye upon him. It was as though his very skin glowed.

CHAPTER 24

Curtis stood in the main hallway. Lunch was over and through the open front doors he could see a half-hearted game of football taking place on the lawn. It was too hot for most of the players; the humid air was like a blanket thrown over them all. He stepped up to the door marked 'private' that separated Mrs Burton-Jones's rooms from the rest of the house. He let the anger he felt bubble up again. It gave him courage. He knocked on the door and waited for a reply.

It didn't come.

He knocked again.

Nothing.

He turned the handle and stepped into her drawing room.

It seemed deserted. The French windows were closed and the air was stifling. It felt more like a greenhouse than a place to sit. He could smell traces of lavender and rose. Maybe Mrs Burton-Jones's perfume? But there was no sign of her.

He moved further into the room. Then stopped. One of the curtains had moved, ever so slightly. As though they had taken a gentle breath.

The room wasn't as deserted as it appeared.

The hairs on the back of his neck tingled. 'Who's here?' Curtis called. 'I know someone's here. Show yourself.'

Show yourself? He was turning into a bad horror film. He pulled himself up straight. 'Whoever you are, you'd better come out.'

The curtain rustled. The yellow satin was pulled back.

'How did you know I was here?' Paige asked, stepping out from behind the curtain. 'Is your sixth sense finally waking up?'

Curtis grinned. 'My sixth sense is absolutely fine. It's a sense called equilibrioception; everyone has it. It lets you know whether you're upright or not. Nothing whatsoever to do with being psychic.'

Paige shook the curtain slightly, to make sure it was hanging straight. 'You're feeling better then,' she said.

'Not really. I found something horrible. Look.' He handed her the photo that he'd brought from his room. She took it and stared.

'Wow. This is really weird. Is this a photo of him? Why's he white?'

Curtis explained what he thought she was looking at *and* why he wanted to see Mrs Burton-Jones.

Paige shook her head. 'She won't tell you anything. Even if she knows. People like her just don't. We've got a neighbour who likes to know everyone else's business; she's always peeping out from behind her curtains. But she never says hello to you in the street, not even if you shout. Mrs Burton-Jones reminds me of her. I think it's the buttoned-up cardies, even though the weather's boiling.'

Curtis took the photo back. 'Well, I have to try something. And if you think talking to her is no use, what are you doing here?'

Paige grinned at him. 'You won't like it. It will score at least an eight on your freak-out-ometer.'

Curtis tried not to smile back. But he couldn't help it. 'Go on, tell me.'

'Well. I was thinking about your dowsing rods. They ripped through the globe like they really wanted to break it. It was about as vicious as a couple of sticks can be.'

'So?'

'And the globe came up in the tarot reading last night. And in the painting, his buttons are globes.

128

Well, I remembered that I'd seen a globe somewhere before. In this room, in fact, when we were told off on our first morning.'

Curtis looked at the object next to the curtain. An old, decorated globe, held up by an elegant wooden stand. He walked over to it. The countries were picked out in beige paint on a watery-blue background. Spidery writing covered the landmasses, the names of countries, cities and towns in a beautiful copperplate. He rested his hand on it. The surface felt wrinkled, as though it had aged. A smart push set it spinning. 'You really believe some spirit guide told you to come and look at this, do you?'

Paige raised an eyebrow. 'Well, it was you holding the dowsing rods. If anything, I think a spirit guide is telling you to come and look at this. And here you are!'

Curtis wondered whether he could explain the concept of coincidence to Paige. No, it would just be a waste of breath. 'So, did you find anything?'

'No. I just got here a second before you. I haven't had a chance to explore yet.' Paige crouched down, examining the globe from every angle. She ran her hands over the sphere, tapping it gently. 'Some globes open up, you know. They're really drinks cabinets in disguise. My uncle has one. But this one doesn't have a latch or anything to open it with.'

'You mean it's a perfectly ordinary globe? What a surprise.'

'Wait! I haven't finished looking.'

Paige tapped the stand with her knuckles. It was made of polished wood, the colour of caramel. Its three legs arched up from the ground to a central stem. A wooden ring, like a little hula hoop around its middle, attached the globe to the stem. Paige tapped the hoop, the stem, two of the legs. The taps sounded flat and solid. Then, as she tapped the third leg, the noise changed. 'You hear that?' she asked.

Instead of a solid sound, it echoed slightly, like tapping a box instead of a log. 'This bit is hollow,' Paige grinned. Her fingers ran over the base, searching for a clasp or a catch. 'Tip it up, I want to see the bottom.'

'I can't, it's too heavy. We'll break it.'

'Do it,' Paige said.

Curtis shrugged, then gripped the top of the stand and pulled it towards him. The globe tipped and began spinning gently. Curtis held tight, straining a little under the weight.

'Good, that's it,' Paige said. 'I can see something. There's a button.' She pressed down.

Curtis heard a sharp click.

CHAPTER 25

Paige felt one side of the leg drop open against her palm – a hidden compartment. She felt a tingle of excitement. She knew it! She leaned down for a better look. A small hole had opened up. It was about the size of a matchbox and she could just waggle her fingertips inside. She felt them brush up against something. It was something delicate, like moths' wings. She gripped whatever it was gently and eased it out. It made a soft, rustling noise as it dropped from its hiding place.

'What is it?' Curtis asked.

'Shh, I'm concentrating.'

Paige pulled whatever it was clear.

Curtis let the globe settle back down on to the floor. Paige wasn't quite sure that it was in exactly the right spot, but it was near enough.

She looked at the object in her hand. It was a piece of paper, folded in quarters. It was stiff and yellow with age. 'Should I open it?'

'Well, it looks like good quality paper, so I should think it will be OK. And anyway, if you don't, I will. The suspense is killing me.'

'On *The Antiques Roadshow* they always use white gloves to handle old paper.' Paige wasn't sure whether the paper would just fall to bits the second she unfolded it.

'Have you got any white gloves?' Curtis asked.

'No.'

'Well then.'

Paige heard a shout from outside in the hallway, then the sound of children running. Break was nearly over. 'What about Mrs Burton-Jones? She might be back any second.'

Curtis looked at the door and then looked at the paper in her hand. 'You're right. I don't want to get caught in here now. Let's read it upstairs.'

He peeped out to check the coast was clear. She followed him out and let the door shut quietly behind her. Phew. No one would know they'd even been there.

The heat was intense at the top of the house. She could feel her T-shirt sticking to her back. She wiped her hands on her jeans; it would be awful to put sweaty hands on the paper.

She sat down on the floor next to Curtis and unfolded it carefully.

There was something written on it. The handwriting was elegant, all swirly with loops at the top of the 'h's and the bottom of the 't's. Like the writing on the globe.

'It's a letter,' Curtis said. 'The address is written at the top. Wickworth Manor. It was written here.'

'Is it from the Wickworth Boy?' Paige leaned in closer. The handwriting was so fancy that it was hard to make out the words. She rushed to the bottom, to read the signature. 'Ver-something. Is it Verity? Who's Verity? Why did the dowsing rods bring us to her?'

'She inherited the house. She was Patience's sister. She was here in 1805 when it all happened. Whatever 'it' was. Here, I think I can read this. It's a bit like my old house master's writing.' Curtis lifted the paper and scanned it for a while; his dark eyes ran back and forth over the lines, then grew wide.

'What does it say?' Paige tugged his sleeve impatiently.

'Listen, I'll read it to you. It's dated 9th April 1866.

"To whosoever finds this letter,

"I know not how to tell this secret that has laid so heavily upon me for what feels like an age, for more than half my lifetime. It is only now, as my own death approaches, that I feel I can speak. No, rather that I must speak. And

133

yet, I do not know who will listen. For I am ashamed and no one who was alive then is still of this world. Perhaps, therefore, this is a prayer. Maybe the souls of those whom I have wronged will hear and forgive.

"'I know, for I hear the servants talk, that already the events of that time are passing into myth. And whose fault is that, if not my own? The truth has not been forgotten, but rather hidden, and by my own hand.'"

Curtis looked up. 'Do you think she means she hid the painting?'

Paige prodded his arm. 'Shh, keep on reading.'

Curtis looked back at the page.

"'My dearest sister Patience was taken from us as she entered the first bloom of womanhood. I cannot speak of the terrible anguish we felt, Father especially. A sickness of the heart and soul struck him upon hearing the dreadful news. He took to his bed, never to rise again.

"'Oh, Father. It is to you that this prayer is offered. You asked something of me that day that I could not do. I could not. The shame would have fallen heavily upon the whole family. Our enemies would have used that shame against us. All would have been lost and men such as Wilberforce and Sharp would have taken it all.

"'But all was lost anyway.

"'Now I know that the shame of breaking my promise was so much worse.

"'I have failed. And now I am too sick to even try. So, I have hidden the one painting in the place where Patience laid her last. All else, in truth, I have commended to our Lord, with the hope that those who should have been honoured will be so in the life hereafter.

"'I am weak. I will hide this prayer too. I will place it inside the globe you loved so much, Father. The globe you brought from the West Indies along with the coach boy, Christopher, whose very name caused me so much shame. I am ready to relinquish this life and submit to judgement in the next.

"'Amen.

"'Verity Burton'"

Curtis put the paper down. 'Wow,' he said.

'Christopher,' Paige said. 'The Wickworth Boy was called Christopher.'

Curtis stood up. He held the letter and moved towards the window. Paige noticed how upright he stood, as though every muscle in his body was tense.

'She sounds like a right piece of work,' Curtis said.

'What do you mean?'

'Wilberforce and Sharp were campaigners against the slave trade.' Curtis's voice sounded tight, angry.

Paige moved to his side, and looked out over the lake. 'So, whatever Verity knew, it would have helped the campaigners? People stayed slaves because she didn't want to be embarrassed? That's horrible.'

Curtis nodded.

'But whatever it was that Verity did, the promise she broke, she felt bad about it. She says so in the letter.'

'Well, that's all right then,' Curtis snapped. 'So long as she's sorry.'

'There's no need to take it out on me.'

There was a pause. 'Sorry,' Curtis said. 'I didn't mean that. I just feel so angry for Christopher. Whatever happened to him was kept a secret for all these years just to stop a family from being embarrassed. We have to find out what happened to him. We have to put this right.'

Paige felt a lump form in her throat. She swallowed it down. 'I want to find out too.'

'Good.' Curtis moved towards the end of the bed, where Christopher's portrait was propped. The photograph of his death mask was there too. Curtis added the letter. 'It's almost a shrine,' he said. Then he turned to face her. 'Any ideas? What should we do next?'

'Well,' Paige said. 'We need to think. But just now we're late for canoeing.'

Curtis smiled. 'I can think and paddle at the same time.'

CHAPTER 26

CJTE/059 Hairbrush and combs, 18th C.

He wondered, sometimes, about the people who rode
inside the coach. The family. Did they notice
the servants around them? The older girl didn't,
of that he was certain. She thought they were
no more than wooden puppets, with no mind or
thoughts behind the dark surface. Sometimes, she
talked as though there was no one but family in
the room to hear. Her maid heard all manner of
indiscretions as she set the girl's hair; brushing,
combing and listening to every word. And all that
was said was quickly common knowledge in the
servants' hall.

But the younger one? It wasn't clear. She
had been heard to say please and thank you.
It was said that as a child she had helped her
nurserymaid with chores, though that seemed

unlikely. She had asked if he would mind rowing her across the lake, she didn't order him to do it. Not that he would have been able to say no, of course, no matter how like a request it seemed.

CHAPTER 27

They were just about to leave his attic when Curtis heard his phone ring. It was Mum's ringtone. He remembered their night-time call, where there had been more silence than words. There was a heavy feeling in his chest as he walked to his open suitcase and fished for the phone.

'Hello?' he said.

'Curtis, it's me,' Mum said. 'Is everything OK?'

Curtis glanced over at Paige. She stood in the doorway, facing the other way, doing her best to look as though she wasn't listening. 'Of course. I can't talk, I'm late for something.'

'Oh, I thought it might be lunchtime. I was hoping to catch you.'

'Why? Is everything OK with you?' Curtis frowned slightly.

'Yes. Yes, it is. But you called so late. I was worried. We thought it might be best to leave you to settle, but maybe we were wrong. Curtis –' Mum paused.

'Yes?'

'Just . . . take care. That's all.'

'OK. Listen, I'm in a hurry.'

'Of course. Well, bye.'

'Bye.'

Curtis ended the call and threw the phone back. He felt as though the room was suddenly colder. He'd managed to forget about Mum and the worry and the disappointment, just for a little while. But now it all washed right back, as though it was a wave that got pulled out on the tide only to crash back to shore moments later.

'What's the matter?' Paige asked.

'Nothing.' How could he explain to Paige? She and her mum were like best friends. She wouldn't understand.

They were the last to arrive at the lake. Mr Appleton gave them a quick nod. Everyone else was pulling on lifejackets and helmets.

'Why does everything we do here mean we wear helmets?' Paige moaned.

Curtis grinned. He pulled his on and clipped it under his chin. Paige picked up a lifejacket and dropped it over her shoulders; its red panels were decorated with go-faster stripes.

'Now, there's not a lot to this,' Mr Appleton said. 'Two to a canoe. You've all got paddles. Try not to soak each other.'

He led them out on to the jetty. Curtis walked beside Paige. He suddenly heard a hiss from behind them.

'Snitch.'

Curtis turned. Liam was there, glaring at Curtis from under the brow of his helmet.

'Pardon?' Curtis asked.

'Snitch,' Liam said, louder this time. 'I've heard what people are saying about me. It was only you who could have told them.'

Curtis stopped walking.

Liam stopped too.

'I don't know what you're talking about.' Curtis tried to think of something he might have done, or said. Anything at all, but his mind was blank.

'Well, new boy, you were the only one who knew. Except for my mates, of course.'

'Knew about what?'

'Don't play innocent with me. I'm no mug.'

'Is there a problem here?' Mr Appleton rested his hands on Curtis's and Liam's shoulders. The weight felt reassuring.

'No, sir,' Liam looked down.

'Well, come on, get paddling.'

The canoe wobbled as Curtis and Paige settled in, but it stayed upright. Curtis leaned towards Paige's back and whispered, 'Any idea what that was all about?'

'Who knows? Sal said at breakfast that Caitlin said that Paul had heard that Liam and his mates were messing around last night, but I don't know what that's got to do with you. Ignore him.'

Curtis watched Liam and his partner move off on to the lake. He remembered Liam's invitation to join in with whatever prank they were getting up to. He'd totally forgotten about it. But obviously Liam hadn't. And someone had tattled. And Curtis was getting the blame for the rumours.

'Forget it,' Paige said.

Curtis wasn't sure that he could, but eventually the gentle rhythm of the paddle pulling through the water settled the anxiety he felt. The glass surface of the lake became a comb of ripples. There were splashes and shouts all around them, but the heat of the sun on the back of his neck, the lap of the water, the call of birds around the lake made it seem tranquil.

'Curtis,' Paige said, twisting around in her seat, 'I've been thinking.'

'Did it hurt?'

'Ha ha. I think Verity's letter proves that the stories about the Wickworth Boy, about Christopher, are true.'

Curtis stopped paddling. Paige had let her paddle drift in the water and their canoe floated with the gentle current.

'I think,' Paige continued, 'I think that if Verity found out that her sister was in love with a slave, then she'd be totally ashamed. And in 1805 William was so furious about it, he packed Patience off and Christopher was locked up. They both died of a broken heart. Then the remorse killed William.'

A waft of humid air pushed their canoe towards the centre of the lake. Curtis wiped the sweat from his forehead with the back of his sleeve. 'You can't die of a broken heart or remorse. I don't know why Christopher and Patience died so close together, but it wasn't that.'

'But what about the stories?'

'They're just stories. Put your paddle back in, we're drifting too far.'

Their canoe was nearer the far bank now than the jetty. The stone chapel he'd noticed on his first day here was much closer. He could see ivy growing across the entrance. He pulled sharply on his paddle and their canoe edged away, back towards the others. Paige followed suit.

'I'm just saying,' she said a bit breathlessly, 'that Verity was ashamed. She said so in the letter. And it would have been shameful, wouldn't it, if your sister fell in love with a slave?'

'We don't know what Verity was ashamed of,' Curtis said quietly. 'It sounded more like she was ashamed of herself than of Patience or Christopher. Her dad asked her to do something and she didn't keep her promise. That's what we need to find out. What didn't Verity do?'

Curtis noticed that the back of Paige's neck was going pink; sunburn. He reached forward and adjusted her hood a bit so that it covered her neck. She twisted in her seat and smiled at him.

He felt a slight jolt as their canoe edged up against the jetty. He held the wooden support while Paige jumped out and tied their rope to the mooring. Curtis lined their paddles up neatly before stepping out. Mr Appleton took in the rest of their equipment. Curtis felt Liam's glare again as he added his lifejacket to the pile. That was another problem he could do without.

'I liked canoeing,' Paige said. 'Turns out we make quite a good team. Now let's see if we can work out what it was that Verity felt so bad about. And I bet you a Curly Wurly it was something to do with love.'

'A Curly Wurly?' Curtis couldn't help but smile.

'It's my favourite. What? Are you scared you'll lose?'

What were the chances of two-hundred-year-old rumours being true? Curtis laughed. The chocolate was practically his already. 'You're on,' he said.

CHAPTER 28

The hall was full of people when they went through for tea. Paige dropped down into a seat opposite Sal and Jo with her tray. She felt pleased that Curtis came and sat next to her.

'The Wickworth Boy is called Christopher and he was in love with someone called Patience,' she told the others.

Sal's forkful of potato stopped midway to her mouth. 'Is that true?' She looked to Curtis for an answer.

'A tiny bit of it is true,' he said. 'Some people called Christopher and Patience lived here once. We don't know they were in love.'

'Oh,' Sal ate her potato.

Paige prodded Curtis with her elbow. 'You're so . . . so . . .'

'Scrupulous?' Curtis suggested. 'Exacting?'

'Annoying,' Paige said.

'I like the idea that a ghost haunts this place looking for his lost love,' Jo said. 'It's romantic.'

'But there's no proof,' Curtis said. 'Just because you like an idea doesn't make it true.'

'I have intuition,' Paige said finally.

Curtis made a snorting noise and shovelled some peas on to his fork. Paige ignored him and took a drink of water.

Through the bottom of her glass, she saw Mrs Burton-Jones walk in. The water made it look as though Mrs Burton-Jones was in a hall of mirrors, with a massive head and a shrivelled body. Then Paige saw the look on Mrs Burton-Jones's face. Paige lowered her glass slowly. The air around Mrs Burton-Jones seemed to crackle and fizz. Paige had a sudden sense of black and orange.

Fury.

Mrs Burton-Jones was angry. Again.

Paige took one more careful sip. What would make Mrs Burton-Jones angry? And why did Paige have such a sinking feeling?

Paige wriggled down in her chair, dropping her eyes to the table. The peas were suddenly very interesting and she concentrated on them hard. A hush spread across the room. Mrs Burton-Jones must have glared everyone into silence.

Paige looked up slowly. It was like trying not to look at a cut on someone's knee; you knew it would be horrible but you had to look anyway.

Mrs Burton-Jones stood near the canteen hatch. All eyes in the room swivelled to look at her. Her lips were pressed together in a thin, white line as she looked around. Her hands were folded across the front of a pink cardie. The knuckles were as white as the pearl buttons that held the cardie closed.

'Boys and girls,' Mrs Burton-Jones said in a voice that was like treacle laced with battery acid. 'Once again I have reason to be disappointed by one among you.

'This afternoon, when I returned to my rooms, I found that an object had been disturbed. This object, of not inconsiderable weight, had been moved. Now, I was forced to consider two alternatives. First, that some ghostly presence had been in my room and shifted my belongings around on a whim.' Nervous laughter broke out near the back of the hall. Mrs Burton-Jones silenced it with a razor glare. 'The second possibility,' she continued, 'is that someone has been into my private rooms and has ransacked them, looking for who on earth knows what.' Her eyes scanned the room, searching out guilty faces. Paige felt her own face flush red and shrank even lower.

'I have considered calling the police,' Mrs Burton-Jones said. 'I considered it, but your teachers assure me that there is no need. They tell me that if I appeal to your better natures, then the culprit will confess and accept their punishment. The alternative,' Mrs Burton-Jones paused, pinching her mouth closed like a dog's bum, 'the alternative is that this week will be cut short and all of you will be sent home immediately while the police investigate the trespass.'

A ripple of horror ran around the room.

'You have tonight to decide. Tomorrow at nine a.m. precisely I will be in my drawing room. I expect the culprit to come and make themselves known to me. Otherwise at nine thirty a.m. you can all begin packing and wait for the coaches to take you home. Your time here will be over.'

Mrs Burton-Jones swept out of the room, like a missile set to kill.

The stunned silence erupted into babble.

'Who was it?'

'What did they do?'

'I bet it was that Liam and his mates.'

'You can't say that. We had nothing to do with it.'

'Bet it was though. Sounds like Liam.'

'What did they steal?'

'Liam, what did you take?'

Silent, in the centre of all the noise, Paige sat with her cheeks burning.

She pressed her fingers to her face, trying to squish away the blush. But it was no good. She was sure she was lit up like a Chinese lantern – glowing with guilt. She sighed. Did she own up and get sent home in disgrace, or, did she keep quiet and get sent home with everyone in disgrace? This was one of the worst decisions she had ever had to make.

She pushed her tray away. Her appetite had vanished.

No one spoke much in Bluebell as they got ready for bed. Paige pulled on her pyjamas and lay down on top of the duvet – it was too hot to lie under it. She could feel Sal and Jo thinking about her; it made the air clammy. They wanted her to confess. Of course they did, they didn't want to get sent home early because of something Paige had done. But they wouldn't tell her to confess, they were her mates, after all. Instead they just lay there, *thinking*.

'Stop thinking,' Paige said. 'I can hear you and you're keeping me awake.'

Sal giggled. 'I knew there had to be a downside to being psychic. Anyway, I wasn't thinking anything bad. I was just wondering what you were going to do, that's all.'

Paige pulled her pillow closer so that it was stuffed right up against her ear. 'Yes, I was wondering that too. Sleep on it, I suppose.'

Paige didn't think she would get to sleep, but she must have done, because the next thing she knew there was the sound of water splashing against the side of a boat. Then she felt the rain, it was lashing down in streams. The oars in her hands were slippery. There was a girl sitting across from her. She wore a long dress that came down to her feet; the silk was soaked. The girl began to shout out, but her words made no sense; they were more like yelps of fear. Paige looked around for the shore, but the sky was too dark to see it. The girl stood up. Paige tried to reach out, to pull her down, but her hands moved too slowly, like pushing through feathers. The boat rocked. Then Paige heard a splash and felt cold water surge up her nose, in her ears, in her mouth.

She woke, panting. Her body was covered in a damp layer of sweat. The duvet underneath her was crumpled. She lay looking up at the darkness, letting the images from her dream fade.

Slowly, her breathing settled and she became aware of another noise. A pattering sound against her window. Rain. The sweltering heat had finally broken and it was raining outside. Was that why she had dreamed of water?

She sat up.

That wasn't it.

It meant something. Her dream meant something. She was sure of it. And if she didn't find out what it was then, come morning, she never would. She would be going home in disgrace and she'd never find out. Paige got out of bed and pulled on her clothes.

'Curtis? Curtis, are you awake?' Paige tapped gently at his door. 'Curtis?'

The door opened slowly and Curtis's head leaned out. His eyes looked swollen shut with sleep. 'What do you want?'

'To see the letter again. Come on, quickly, we haven't got all night.'

Paige pushed past him and flicked on the light switch. Curtis shielded his eyes. 'What's going on?'

'We've got until tomorrow morning to find out whether Patience and Christopher were in love.'

'And what promise Verity broke,' Curtis said.

'So I'm not going to sleep through the last few hours we have here.'

Curtis nodded and rubbed his face with both hands. 'You're right. We'll have to own up in the morning. We have to. We should use the time we have left. Might as well be hanged for a sheep as a lamb.'

Paige peered at him. 'What? What sheep?'

He grinned. 'Nothing. Let's look at the letter again. There might be something we missed.' He took it from the corner of the picture frame, then smoothed it out and began re-reading. Paige looked over his shoulder.

'Ooh,' Paige said. 'I've just realised that she hid the painting in "the place where Patience laid her last"; that's your bed. Yuck.'

Apart from the fact that Curtis had been sleeping on someone's deathbed, there was nothing else in the letter that Paige hadn't noticed before. 'It's really annoying,' she said. 'It's like Verity wants someone to know about what happened, but she doesn't want to have to spell it out.'

Curtis folded the letter up and put it back in the frame. 'I suppose that's what it's like when you're ashamed. You want people to know what you've done, but you can't find the words to say it.'

Paige felt a spurt of anger in her chest. 'Well, Verity has had it her own way for too long. She knew something that could have changed people's lives for the better and she did nothing about it. It's time for her to tell the truth and we're going to make her.'

CHAPTER 29

'Verity Burton has been dead for well over a hundred years,' Curtis said. 'How do you plan on making her do anything?'

'Being dead isn't the end, you know. There are ways of getting in touch with anyone. You just have to know what you're doing.'

Of course, that was always her answer: ghosts and ghouls and things that go bump. He should have known. In the morning this would all be over, one way or another, and she wanted to raise the dead. Well, so did he, but he wanted to do it for real. He wanted to find out the truth. A boy had been brought to Wickworth Manor from the West Indies as a slave. He had worked here until his death. The nature of that death was deliberately hidden by his owner. Why? Because somehow it would have helped other slaves.

Only the truth mattered now.

Curtis shivered.

'It's getting cold,' Paige said. 'You should put on a jumper.'

It was true; he could hear the wind outside. It blew hard now, whipping rain in gravel pellets against the windowpane. 'I don't want to do a seance or anything like that,' he said. 'I want the truth.'

Paige threw a jumper at him. 'So do I. And dowsing got us the letter, remember? That was my idea. So, unless you can come up with something else, stop moaning and help me.'

There had to be something better than Paige's mumbo-jumbo. Back to the library? Or the internet? No. There was nothing on the web about this. Curtis rested his hand on the edge of the painting; the frame was slightly warm to the touch, as though the wood was alive. 'OK,' he said. 'I'll help, but only until something more effective occurs to me.'

'That'll do. We're going to need supplies. Talc or flour, to draw the sacred shape. You can see footprints of spirits if they walk through the talc. We'll need a thermometer. Has your fancy phone got one?'

'No, I don't think so.'

'Where can we get one? Have you got any talc in your washbag?' Paige stepped towards his suitcase.

'No! Of course I don't have talc,' he said stepping between her and the case. 'Do I look like someone's grandma? Look, there's probably flour in the kitchen. And Carol might have a thermometer too. We should check there. And give me a second to change out of my pyjamas.'

Paige nodded. 'Good idea. Only fools raise the dead in their pyjamas.'

Curtis followed Paige downstairs. They both stayed close to the side wall, careful to tread on the edge of each step so that each footfall was absolutely silent. In the main hall the sound of the wind was louder, battering at the front door. It was a night for raising the dead all right.

The refectory was deserted, with tables laid out ready for breakfast. Paige paused. Curtis realised that she'd never been in the kitchen before. 'It's this way,' he said and opened the door at the side of the serving hatch.

Apart from the clinical glow of the fly-zapper, the kitchen was dark; no moon shone in through the windows as the storm clouds were too low.

'I'll find the thermometer,' Paige said. 'You get the flour.'

Curtis shook his head. How was he getting sucked into another of Paige's crazy ideas?

She pulled open a stainless-steel drawer. It squeaked horribly. He watched her pull out plastic food bags and loose pens and some sticky labels, but no thermometer. She glanced at him. 'Flour!'

'OK, OK.' He knew where to look. The pantry was stuffed full of sacks: rice, pasta and, tucked right at the back, a sack of white flour. 'Got it,' he called back towards the kitchen.

'Bingo!' Paige said. 'I've got a thermometer.' She held up a metal prong with a square of white plastic at the end. 'My gran's got one of these for prodding into joints of meat to check they're ready.' She switched it on. 'The temperature is nineteen degrees.'

Curtis scooped some flour into an empty mayonnaise tub and pressed on a lid. 'Now what?'

'Now we wake Verity.'

CHAPTER 30

This was going to be dangerous. Mum would hit the roof and keep right on going into space if she ever found out. Paige wondered if she should warn Curtis. Not that he believed in it anyway. A summoning wasn't the same as a seance. It was much more serious. She would be calling a soul against its will. It could be angry, violent. It might even bring others with it.

But it had to be done. If Verity was ever going to tell the truth about Christopher and Patience, then tonight was the night it had to happen.

'Where are we going?' Curtis asked as she held open the kitchen door. 'Back to my room? Or the old stable?'

'No,' Paige said. 'The best place to do this is where Verity is now. We have to find her grave.'

Curtis grabbed her arm. 'You're not serious!'

'Of course I am.' Paige shrugged her shoulders and pulled her arm free. 'Her bones will channel her energy. We need to find her grave. Let's start at the chapel.'

Curtis clasped the tub of flour to his chest. His lips were pulled together tightly. He shook his head. 'No way. I'm not digging up some old bones. That's not right. If Mrs Burton-Jones finds out we're digging up her ancestors, then she'll call the police. There's probably some law against it. We'll go to jail. Then my mum really will stop talking to me. Forget it, it's not happening.'

Paige turned to look at him. His eyes looked wild in the darkness. He was scared. *He's right to be*, a small voice inside her whispered. They were playing with fire. Not to mention how angry Mrs Burton-Jones would be. And Curtis's mum and dad. And everyone at school if they all got sent home early. This was really a terrible way to make a new start at a new school.

But that was no reason to chicken out.

'Curtis,' Paige said. 'We don't have to dig up bones, I promise. Just be near them. It's about the energy, you know, religious places have power we can tap into. Her energy will be nearby, especially as we know she was religious. Remember what she wrote in her letter? That it was a prayer and that she was commanding the truth to God?'

'Not com*mand*ing, she was com*mend*ing it to the Lord, –' Curtis stopped. His mouth dropped open and his eyebrows shot up.

'Curtis, are you all right?' Paige asked.

'Yes! Yes, of course! Paige, you're a genius.' Curtis grinned, 'You're brilliant. The letter *was* a clue. She did tell us where to find the rest of the story. She *commended it to the Lord*. She gave it to God to look after. And where would you put something that you wanted God to look after?'

Paige grinned back. 'The chapel!'

'Exactly. Turns out your plan isn't so daft after all. Let's go. But we shouldn't go out by the front door, we might wake Mrs Burton-Jones. We should go out by the back.'

The door that led out into the courtyard was locked, but a huge key hung on a piece of string next to it. Curtis moved to open it.

'I knew it.' A voice spoke behind Paige. She spun round. Liam.

What was he doing here?

'I knew it would be you two.' Liam stepped closer. Paige could see that his face was crumpled up in anger.

'Us two what?' Paige asked.

'You two running around, breaking things, stealing things. Whatever it was you did in Mrs Burton-Jones's

159

rooms. I knew it would be you letting me take the blame.'

Curtis left the back door and came to stand beside Paige. Liam swaggered closer.

'You and your pet snitch,' Liam said.

Curtis pulled himself up tall. He and Liam were both shrouded in long shadows. They looked like boxers facing up to each other in an alley somewhere. Paige felt her heartbeat quicken. There couldn't be a fight now. If they woke any of the teachers, this would all be over.

She stepped between them.

'Liam, I don't know what you think we've been doing, but we haven't got you into any trouble.'

'Oh yeah? Everyone's talking about me. I've heard them. Saying I was messing around the other night and that I was the one who broke into that lady's room. Everyone always thinks it's me whenever anything goes wrong. And that snitch has made it worse.'

Curtis stepped closer. He edged Paige out of the way. 'I didn't tell anyone about that conversation we had. No one, not even Paige. I'm not a snitch.'

'Well someone is. And of all the people who knew, you're the one I don't trust. I'm going to be sent home tomorrow, I know it. I thought I'd be able to start at secondary school with new teachers and new classmates and no reputation. But you ruined that. You think just because you're posh it's OK for someone else to take the blame for what you do?'

'I don't think that,' Curtis whispered.

Liam jabbed the air with his finger. 'Well, let's see how you like a taste of your own medicine. I won't take the blame. I won't. I'm going to get Miss Brown right now and she can see who's really wandering around where they shouldn't.'

Paige stepped closer. 'No, Liam, please.'

'Oh, it's please now, is it? Well, tough. I'm not going to be sent home tomorrow just so you can run around having fun. I'm going to tell. See how you like being snitched on.'

'You wouldn't. You're not a snitch.'

Liam paused. 'You think?'

'I know,' Paige said. 'You wouldn't do something like that.'

'Shows what you know. Watch me.' Liam spun around on his heels and stormed out of the kitchen. He slammed a metal countertop on the way out, then he was gone.

Curtis looked at her, his eyes dark with worry. 'Will he do it?'

She shook her head. 'No, no way. He's no snitch.' She paused. 'But maybe we should hurry. Just in case.'

She pushed open the back door. At once she was hit by a wall of rain; it lashed into the ground so hard that drops bounced back up. 'Should have brought a brolly,' she said and then stepped outside.

She was drenched in an instant. Curtis too. But there was something exciting about being out in midsummer, in the middle of a storm. Paige whooped and raced to the side of the house. It would be a long walk around the lake to get to the chapel and they didn't have much time.

'Wait,' Curtis said.

'What? We have to hurry.'

'I know.' He ran over to the equipment shed. 'But the quickest way to get from A to B is a straight line. We should go across the lake. We'll need lifejackets.'

The canoes? Was Curtis crazy? Maybe. But he was right. It would be quicker.

He was already undoing the bolt and pulling the door open by the time she reached him. The room was pitch dark. He fumbled for the light switch. It lit up rows of lifejackets, helmets, ropes, harnesses, map cases and compasses. Curtis grabbed a jacket and helmet and threw them towards her before grabbing some for himself.

'Helmets? Really?' Paige asked.

'We're breaking into a chapel in the middle of the night when we've been expressly told to mind our own business. We're getting there by canoe in a storm. The least we can do is observe good Health and Safety,' he said with a grin.

Paige pulled on the equipment. The dash to the lake was better – the rain dripped off the peak of her helmet and didn't run in horrible streams down her neck. The lifejacket kept her body dry, though her arms were covered with goosebumps.

Curtis dropped the tub of flour into the canoe, then lowered himself in after it. The seats were wet and puddles of water were forming in the bottom. Paige got in too and grabbed a paddle. Cold water seeped in through the seat of her jeans. High winds made the choppy waves spray up on to her face. The canoe was nowhere near as steady as it had been earlier. Curtis pulled hard with his paddle, pushing them into the middle of the dark water. The sound of the rain hitting the surface was like hundreds of snakes hissing.

A light flashed across the churning lake. Paige turned to look. A car swept up the drive; its headlights panned across the front of the house. The lights left a green after-image in Paige's eyes. Who was driving to Wickworth Manor at this time of night?

'Paige!' Curtis yelled. 'Paddle!'

Paige pulled hard. Their paddles were on opposite sides of the canoe, dragging them forward into the darkness.

Had Liam really snitched? Had Mrs Burton-Jones called the police? She'd thought a lot of bad things about Liam, but she'd never have believed that he was a snitch.

'Faster!' Curtis cried.

They powered through the water. They were in the centre now, far from the banks on either side.

Suddenly, a shaft of lightning split the sky. A roll of thunder followed seconds later. Paige gasped. Heavy drops of rain hurled against her cheeks.

Then another bolt hit and cast an electric glow around the chapel. 'The Tower!' Paige shouted.

'What?' Curtis's voice was almost drowned out by the noise of the storm.

'It looks like The Tower! The tarot card. I saw this on our first day here. Change. Destruction. It's coming true.' This was a sign. They were on the right path, she knew it. Paige paddled even harder, carving great chunks out of the water to speed up the canoe. Her shoes splashed in deep puddles at the bottom of the boat.

The bank was close. There was no jetty on this side, just reeds and grass and the roll of the waves. 'We'll have to jump out. There's no mooring,' Curtis yelled over his shoulder.

Paige was glad of the lifejacket now. She felt the canoe scrape against a rock or something hidden below the surface, then it jolted to a stop near the bank.

Curtis threw the mayonnaise tub on to dry land. He took hold of the rope and stood up. 'Hold on tight,' he said.

Paige gripped the sides of the canoe while he leapt. It wobbled underneath her, ready to tip over. But Curtis landed on the bank and held the rope taut, steadying the canoe. Then, it was her turn.

Another bolt of white light crackled through the sky. The thunder boomed. The centre of the storm was near. There was a current of electricity in the air that made her mouth taste metallic and her hair prickle under her helmet. She stood up. It seemed like miles to the bank. She took a deep breath and jumped.

Curtis grabbed her wrist and pulled her forward; they both fell on to the wet bank. Mud splashed on her clothes and face. But she was safe. For now.

'Let's get out of the rain,' Curtis said, heading towards the chapel.

The door was shrouded in dripping ivy; it smelled green and earthy. She pushed the ivy aside. Curtis took the door handle in both hands and turned. The old lock squealed in protest, but it turned and the door opened.

Before they stepped into the darkness of the chapel, Paige gave one last glance back at the house. She thought she could see figures standing in the driveway, but the rain was battering down so hard that it was impossible to make out who it was. She just had to hope that they had enough of a head start.

The chapel was small inside, though the roof stretched high above them. The two sides of the building were studded with windows. Despite this, it was dark and her eyes took a minute to get used to the gloom. There was hardly any furniture – the pews were long gone, and just the stone altar at the far end and a few chairs arranged against a side wall remained.

Now that she was out of the rain, she realised how cold she was. Paige tugged off the helmet and lifejacket. She rubbed her arms, then kept her hands clamped to her shoulders. Her jeans and trainers squelched as she walked.

'Do you think we should look for a graveyard?' she asked. 'We need to find where Verity's buried.'

'If you commended something to God, you'd do it inside the chapel, I think. Let's look around. I've got a torch on my phone.' Curtis patted down his pocket and then pulled it out. 'Oh,' he said. 'Two missed calls from Mum. Why's she ringing so late?'

Paige sighed. 'She cares about you, you know.'

'You can't possibly know that.' Curtis's voice was quiet. She had to strain to hear him against the wind. 'You're just guessing again.'

'Am I? Listen, when we get out of this, promise me you'll call your mum.'

'Mrs Burton-Jones will be calling both our mums, most likely.'

'Promise,' Paige said, glaring at him.

Curtis looked down. 'Fine. I'll call her, I promise.'

'Good. Now that that's settled, let's do this.'

Paige took the tub from Curtis and opened it. A small cloud of flour puffed from the top. 'I've seen this in one of my mum's books,' she said. 'I need to draw a circle on the ground with the flour. Then you say special words inside the circle. I'm pretty sure I remember what to say.'

Her hands were trembling as she looked around for the best place to do the ritual. She tried to ignore the fear eating away inside her.

Maybe over by the altar?

She stepped towards it, then Curtis cried out.

'Hey,' he said. His torch shone against one of the side walls. 'Hey, look at this.'

'This' was a sandstone slab set into the wall. As Paige got closer, she saw that there were black letters cut into the grey stone.

'"*In Memoriam. William Burton 1742–1805*",' Curtis read, tracing the words with his fingertips. '"*His beloved wife Catherine Burton 1763–1793 and their dear daughter Patience Burton 1792–1805*". And this one, right next to it, says "*Verity Burton 1791–1866. Rest In Peace*".' He stepped back. 'Here they are; the whole family alongside each other.'

'How can those three all fit in there?' Paige looked at the space, about the size of a flat-screen TV.

'I guess they're just all squished on top of each other,' Curtis said.

'Gross. Why are they buried inside the chapel anyway? Shouldn't they be in a graveyard?'

Curtis shrugged. 'People are sometimes. Especially if the chapel belongs to them.'

Paige looked at the inscription. This was the perfect spot. Verity, Patience and William were all here. It was only Christopher who was missing. She shook the flour from the tub turning in a circle as she did so. The flour looked bone-white against the dusty floor. She took the kitchen thermometer from her pocket. 'It's fourteen degrees,' she said.

She looked at Curtis and took a deep breath. She was really going to do this. It was all up to her now.

CHAPTER 31

Curtis watched Paige step into the white circle she'd made on the floor. She began whispering to herself. He wasn't certain whether this was a spell she had read somewhere, or something she'd made up herself. Either way the chances of it resulting in any useful information were somewhere between nil and absolute zero.

Their success or failure was up to him. He had an icy cold feeling in his stomach. He recognised it. Fear. The same feeling he'd had when he'd sat down in the huge exam hall at Northdene. The same feeling he'd had when he'd had to tell Mum and Dad that their dreams for him were over.

'Curtis!' Paige called. 'The thermometer's dropping. Twelve degrees. Now eleven. It's getting colder.'

'There's a storm,' he said. 'The temperature is bound to drop.'

'No,' she said. 'It's working. The spirits are close; I can feel them.'

Curtis shone his phone at the memorial. He ran his fingers along the carved lettering. The grains of sandstone were rough against his fingertips. Outside, the sound of the rain hitting the roof was louder. But there was something else too – shouts? Were there people outside?

He glanced back at Paige, who was concentrating on the thermometer in her hand. Had she heard the calls?

Curtis stepped away from the stone. If Mrs Burton-Jones or the police were close enough for him to hear them shouting, then they didn't have much time. He was going to be sent down again, he just knew it. He was going to have to explain to Mum that he had messed up. It had been hard to tell her the first time. Well, not hard, impossible. He hadn't been able to say the words aloud. *I failed.* He hadn't said them to anyone, but he had thought them over and over again until it was like listening to his own breathing.

He couldn't fail again.

Verity had been the last person to know the truth. She must have left them a clue.

'Verity,' Paige whispered. 'Verity, come to us now and share your secrets.'

Verity had *wanted* someone to know. That's why she had left the letter in the globe. She had been ashamed of her secret, but she hadn't wanted it to die with her.

'Are you there? Speak to us, Verity.'

Curtis swept his light along the walls; it reflected back off the dirty windows and seeped into the shadowy stone. Verity must have left a clue. She *must*.

And then he saw a glint of gold.

He swung the beam of light back.

Some six metres above the floor of the chapel was an alcove. Inside the alcove stood a statue decorated with gold fragments.

'What is that?' Curtis whispered.

Paige stopped whispering and looked up.

The statue was of a man, bent double, carrying a child on his back. The child held up a globe; slivers of gold leaf still shone from its circumference.

'A gold globe. Like the buttons on Christopher's red coat,' Curtis said.

'St Christopher,' Paige said.

'What?'

'That's St Christopher, the patron saint of travellers. Mum gave me a St Christopher medal when I started going to school on my own. He keeps you safe. That's the baby Jesus he's carrying.'

Curtis felt a tingling on the nape of his neck. St Christopher. Verity *had* left them a clue. 'That's it! Up there. We have to get up there,' Curtis said.

'No way.'

'Look at St Christopher. Look at his face. It's black.'

'How can you tell in the dark? Maybe it's just dusty.'

'No, I'm right. Verity left a trail and we're hot on it!'

Paige looked at the flour circle at her feet. Curtis could see the whites of her eyes, open in amazement. 'Look! The flour, it's moved!' Part of the flour circle had been disturbed; a small section now fanned outwards. 'It . . . worked,' she said. 'I asked Verity to come and tell us her secret and she did. She told you!'

'No. She didn't. I saw it for myself.'

'But the flour!'

'It was just the wind. Now, come on.'

Curtis ran his palm along the wall. The alcove was set high up and the stone below was smooth. 'We need something to climb on.'

Paige looked up at the wall. 'You want me to climb all the way up there? Forget it.'

'Fine. I'll go up and you can keep a lookout.' Curtis scanned the chapel. Maybe a chair would do. He grabbed one and pulled it over; its legs rasped along the stone floor.

Paige leapt out of her circle and ran to the entrance. 'Oh, yikes! There are lights on all over the house. And more moving around the lake. They'll be here any minute.'

Curtis felt the cold feeling in his stomach spread. If he didn't find something soon, he'd be sent home from a school he hadn't even started at, and all for nothing.

He scrambled up on to the chair. It wobbled a bit, but didn't topple over. His face was close to the stone wall; he could feel the cold and damp of the chapel on his skin, the air smelling dusty and peppery in his nose.

He stretched up. St Christopher was still out of reach. But his fingers brushed something: an indentation in the smoothness of the stone. His fingers slotted into it perfectly, as though it was there for that purpose. He reached up with his left hand. There was another indentation, slightly higher up. There were handholds! They started high up, so that no one would notice them from the ground, but they had been put there deliberately. He grinned, despite the fact that he was on tiptoe high above a stone floor.

Curtis jammed his fingers into the holes and heaved himself up. His feet scrabbled for purchase against the smooth stone. Friction held him in place – just. He reached up and found another groove. He was climbing now; creeping closer to the statue. Dust and small

173

grains of stone fell to the ground as he climbed. His breathing grew ragged and his fingertips felt raw where they gripped the wall. But the statue was getting closer.

'Quick!' Paige yelled. 'They're nearly here!'

Curtis stretched his arm nearly out of its socket and grabbed St Christopher's ankle, which held firm. He swung himself into the alcove, which was the size of a small cupboard. He had to hunch down, but there was just enough room for him to balance next to the statue.

He ran his hands around the space, searching for a shelf or a box, or a loose cover, or *something*.

There was nothing.

There *couldn't* be nothing.

He had been so sure that there would be something here. He couldn't fail now, not when he was so close. His fear swelled. He felt as though the space inside the alcove was shrinking, that he was being pinned down, crushed. They would be caught and that would be the end of it. He'd be sent home, like Northdene all over again.

No.

He wouldn't give up, not this time; he wouldn't just sit there and wait for the end. This time it would be different. He felt around the alcove again, worming his fingers into every crack and groove. But there was just the saint, the baby he carried and the globe.

The globe.

Curtis took out his phone and shone the light on to the statue. The gold decoration on the globe shone like sweet wrappers. But he could see now that the gold didn't pick out the shapes of continents, and it wasn't a random pattern either.

It was an arrow.

It pointed clockwise around the circumference of the sphere.

Curtis held the globe with both hands and twisted. It gave slightly, with a grating noise. Then it stopped. Jammed. He tried again, like trying to twist the top off a jam jar. But it wouldn't move.

'Paige!' he said. 'Paige, you have to get up here, I need help.'

Paige ran lightly over from the doorway. She stood below him, looking up. 'I can't get up there, I can't.'

'You have to. I can't do this by myself, I'm not strong enough.'

'Neither am I! I'd rather get caught.'

Curtis felt a surge of anger. It was all right for her, she had a mum who didn't mind if she did something wrong. Paige's mum would never be disappointed in her. 'You have to, Paige. There's no choice.'

'Yes there is. We can both run and hide. It might be OK. It's only our word against Liam's.'

'Yes and Mrs Burton-Jones doesn't like us; she could easily believe Liam. Take a deep breath and get up here.'

Paige frowned, then reached for the back of the chair. She pulled herself up so that she was standing on the seat.

'That's it, you can do it.'

She reached up slowly.

Outside, the noise of shouts was much clearer now. Curtis was sure that he could make out Liam's voice. Paige's breath came in shallow gasps. Her fingers crawled across the wall searching for the handholds. She made a noise that was somewhere close to whimpering.

'I can't.'

She wasn't going to do it. They would be caught like this, with nothing to show for it but a ton of trouble. Curtis could have screamed in frustration. All she needed to do was to move.

'Paige. Listen to me. Those spirits you believe in, they need you to do this. They're counting on you. I'm counting on you. All you have to do is put one hand up, then the other. But you have to do it and you have to do it now.'

Her hand moved. It found the first handhold, then the next. She was getting closer. Curtis reached down and grabbed the back of her shirt. He heaved. She scrambled into the alcove and sat, gasping, on the edge.

He grinned at her. She gave a shaky laugh. 'Hello,' she said.

'You were brilliant. Now, grab hold of this globe and twist.'

Their hands interlocked over the sphere, her pale hands over his dark ones. The globe made a tight, grinding sound. It turned right round. Curtis heard a crisp click at the back of the alcove. A small door opened up.

He shone his torch into the dark space. 'Come on,' he said and slipped inside.

CHAPTER 32

The only light came from Curtis's phone and Curtis was between his phone and Paige. So she could see hardly a thing beyond the small doorway. But the answer to Verity's secret was ahead, and an angry Miss Brown was behind – not to mention Mrs Burton-Jones. Paige took a deep breath and followed. The space was low and narrow. They had to crawl in.

'Be careful,' he whispered, 'there are steps.'

They were so steep, she had to climb down backwards. She eased down after him, her fingers gripped the cold edge of each stone tightly. It was like dropping into a well. She could hear Curtis breathing hard below her as he made his way down. She shivered. The spirits wanted them here. The spirits were helping. She had to believe that. If the spirits weren't friendly, then she and Curtis were being led down into who knows what and not a single living soul knew where to look for them. If the door above closed behind them, they would be trapped in the dark. Alone with the spirits. Paige felt a surge of panic. She bit her lip and tasted the metallic tang of blood.

Ahead of her, Curtis stopped. Paige banged into his back.

'It's a dead end,' he said.

'What? It can't be.'

'It is. It's just a stone wall.'

Paige could hear Curtis's fingers rasping over the wall. Quick flashes of light from the torch showed dark rows of stone like the clenched teeth of a giant.

A sound came from above. A solid click. She only noticed that there had been a draught of air from above now that it stopped. The doorway had closed.

There was a dead end in front of them. And the way out was closed behind them. And the walls on all four sides were tighter than a chimneybreast. They were trapped.

Paige gasped. She felt as though strong arms had clamped themselves around her chest. She sucked in air, but her lungs wouldn't fill. She heard a distant roaring in her ears, growing louder. Her hands flew to her throat, which tightened shut. She slumped to her knees.

Curtis squeezed down next to her. She could see his mouth moving, but she couldn't hear his words. The only sound in the whole world was the roaring inside her own ears.

Her head dropped forward; she was curled in a tight ball. The smell of soil and decay was strong.

Tears rolled down her cheeks, dripping on to the earth.

Then the light from the phone went out.

She froze, her eyes desperately trying to make out shapes. Nothing.

Then, in the darkness, she realised she could feel something.

Air on her cheeks.

Where was that coming from?

She tried to lift her head. It felt as heavy as rocks. But she managed to wriggle closer to the source of the draught. There was definitely air coming from the bottom of the solid wall in front of them. She reached out with a shaking hand. Her fingers passed under the wall, into blackness. There was a gap. The wall didn't go right the way down.

Paige blinked a few times, trying to clear the fuzziness. She lifted her head, her shoulders; she pushed herself until she was sitting up.

'Are you OK?' Curtis asked. 'I think you fainted. There may not be enough oxygen in here. Which is bad news. We need to get out. If we climb back up, we can try to get the door open. Or we can shout, maybe Liam and the others will hear us. Maybe.'

Paige laid her hand on his arm. 'There's a gap at the bottom of the wall. See.' Paige reached out and stretched her hand into the darkness. 'It's small, but we can probably wriggle through.'

Curtis whistled slowly. 'Paige, you're brilliant.' He paused. 'Only –'

'What?'

'Are you sure you want to go through? Think about it. We climbed up above the memorial. Then dropped down behind it. If we crawl under there, we'll come out inside their tomb.'

Paige shivered. Was Curtis right? It was hard to know which direction they were facing in the darkness. Were the bodies of the Burton family mouldering there on the other side of the wall?

She felt the hair on the back of her neck stand up. They were going to have to do it, crawl into a space with dead bodies. She didn't know if she could, not even for Christopher. Not even for Curtis.

He bent down and shone his phone into the gap at the bottom of the wall.

'Can you see . . . skeletons?' Paige asked.

'I don't think so. I can see something though.' He lay down and crawled his way under the wall. Now

Paige was left alone in the dark. She took one look back. It was so black that she couldn't make out the stairs any more. If she didn't go after Curtis, she would be stuck in this horrible dark well for ever. No way was she doing that. She took a deep breath, then forced herself to follow.

She was in a small space, even smaller than the one she'd climbed in from. She lifted herself into a crouching position, waiting to hear a sickening crunch as her feet trod on bone. But there was nothing. Only Curtis, breathing close to her ear.

'What did you see?' she asked.

He swivelled the light around. 'No bodies. But there is that.'

The light shone on a wrapped something in the middle of the space. It was squarish, with rounded edges, swaddled in cloth. A thick envelope leaned against the object.

'Commended to the Lord,' Curtis whispered. 'This is what Verity wanted to keep secret.'

Paige reached out to touch it, but a cry made her freeze.

'Curtis! Paige!' The call came from nearby. Someone was on the other side of the memorial stone. 'Curtis! Can you hear me?'

The phone clattered from Curtis's hand and went dark. 'Mum?' he said. 'Mum! Mum!'

'Curtis? Where are you?'

'Here! We're in here!' He banged against the heavy stone with the flat of his hands. Paige banged hard too. Clouds of dust flew up into her mouth and eyes.

'Curtis?' The cry was more like a wail now, desperate and cold.

'Mum!'

The stone in front of them groaned.

'It moved!' Paige said. 'It moved. Here, quick.' She grabbed Curtis's shoulder and pulled him back so that they were both sitting down. She raised her feet and pushed them as hard as she could against the slab of stone. 'Help me.'

Curtis lifted his feet too and together they strained against it. It was definitely moving now, inching forward. There was a squeal of rock against rock. Dust swirled. And then a chink of pale light.

'We're nearly there!'

One last heave and the stone slid out and crashed to the ground.

A strong torch beam shone on her face, then flicked over to Curtis. 'Curtis,' a woman's voice whispered. 'You're OK. Oh, thank God, you're OK.'

The woman reached out and half pulled, half lifted Curtis from the space.

'Mum,' he said and fell into her hug. Then he stood upright. He was nearly as tall as her. 'Mum, what are you doing here?'

Curtis's mum made a noise that was somewhere between crying and laughing. She pulled him back into her arms.

Paige lowered herself from the hole they'd made in the wall. The memorial was on the floor, broken in half. Flour and dust had risen up giving the air a milky colour. She could feel it settling on her skin and hair. Paige lifted the wrapped object and the envelope down from the place where they had been hidden for nearly a hundred and fifty years. Curtis's phone winked at her. She took that too.

'Curtis, do you want to see what it is?' she asked, holding up the object.

He turned towards her. 'Yes. Yes, of course.'

But his mum held up her hand. 'You must be Paige, yes?' Paige nodded. 'Well, Paige, we are not doing anything until we've got back to the house and into some dry clothes. I want to know what you both were playing at going out on a lake in a storm, but only when you're both safe.'

Paige felt sick at the thought of going to face Miss Brown and Mrs Burton-Jones and even Liam, but it had to be done. And at least they had Verity's secret, even if they didn't know what it was yet.

She followed Curtis and his mum out into the night. The rain had turned into a fine mist and heavy drops plopped down from the trees. It smelled clean, like fresh laundry. Curtis leaned against his mum and she took his arm to steady herself on the wet path. 'We'll take the long way back,' she called. 'No more canoes.'

Paige gripped the object tightly and followed the torch beam and the two figures back around the lake.

CHAPTER 33

Mum was here. Curtis couldn't believe it. How was she here? Why? Her hand was laced through his arm; he could feel the weight of it in the crook of his elbow as they stumbled along the path.

'I thought something awful might have happened to you,' she said into the dripping dark. 'I got here and no one knew where you were. The awful woman who owns the place didn't even know where your room was. The boys you were meant to be with had never even seen you. And you didn't answer your phone. Curtis, I thought . . . I thought, well, awful things.'

'I'm sorry. I didn't know you were here.'

'I had to come.'

Curtis waited for Mum to explain. Paige stomped along behind them, but she was too far back to hear.

'Those calls from you,' Mum said, 'they broke my heart. You sounded so unhappy here. I couldn't stand it any more. I had to see you. I know I've let you down.'

Curtis almost stumbled. 'You? *You* let *me* down?'

'Yes, I know I did. We should have tried harder. We should have found a way to keep you at Northdene. It's all my fault. Well, we will find a way, I promise. I'll get a new job, and an evening job too. Dad as well. Bar work, or cleaning, or something. We'll get enough money together so that you can go back. I can't bear it that you're so unhappy.'

'No!' Curtis couldn't help but shout. 'No, it was my fault. I was the one who failed. I had my chance and I didn't take it. It was me who failed the scholarship exam, not you.'

Mum's hand squeezed his elbow. 'But we put too much pressure on you.'

'No. I failed. But it's OK. I swear it is. I don't want to go back. I want to stay here.'

'Are you sure?' Something like a sob caught in Mum's throat.

'I'm sure. If they'll let me.' They were close to the house now and he could see people on the driveway. Lots of them were still in their pyjamas and dressing gowns, others had phones clamped to their ears or torches in their hands. Mum moved towards one of the grown-ups to call off the search.

Liam stepped away from a group of boys. His swagger wasn't as pronounced as usual.

'I didn't do all this,' Liam said, waving towards the crowd. 'They all got up and started looking for you anyway. I didn't snitch. I couldn't.'

Curtis looked at Liam whose dark eyes shone with emotion. Curtis nodded; Liam needed a fresh start just as much as he did himself. 'I know. It was my mum. She woke everyone up.'

'Oh, right.'

'And Liam, I didn't snitch either. I promise.'

Liam nodded. 'OK, new man.'

'You can call me Curtis. If you want.'

'OK, Curtis.'

Paige appeared by his side, still carrying the bundle. 'What are you doing out here? There's a firing squad to face,' she said.

'We're in trouble, aren't we?'

'Yup.'

'We're going to be sent home?'

'Yup.'

'Shame,' Liam said. 'I was just starting to like you.'

Ten minutes later Curtis found himself in dry clothes, with a cup of hot chocolate, standing in the middle of Mrs Burton-Jones's drawing room.

He had carried the portrait of Christopher down from his room. Now, it was propped up on the sofa. Paige leaned the wrapped object next to it. They were roughly the same size and shape.

'I think you'd better tell us exactly what's been going on,' Mrs Burton-Jones said in a quiet voice.

'I think that's an excellent idea,' Miss Brown said.

Curtis nodded. He looked at Mum. She was smiling at him, but it was a pinched smile, worried. He knew she would take some convincing.

Paige came and stood next to him. He could see flecks of grey rubble in her blonde hair. There was a streak of dirt across her face. He must look as bad. But there was no mistaking the huge grin on her face. She held the final clue – the envelope that had been hidden in the chapel – and she was ready to be sent home in disgrace, if that was the price they had to pay.

Curtis cleared his throat. 'This is Christopher,' he said. 'He came here from the West Indies. He was a slave. We don't know when he arrived, but he died in 1805. The same year as Patience Burton, and her father, William. Verity Burton inherited the estate and hid the truth about their deaths.'

'Christopher and Patience were in love,' Paige interjected. 'He's the Wickworth Boy.'

'We don't *know* that they were in love. We just know that there was something Verity didn't want anyone to find out. We hope –' he paused as he realised how much he wanted it, '– we hope that we've found the true story in the chapel tonight.'

He put his mug down carefully and then walked over to the sofa. He took the cloth wrapping in his hand and lifted it gently. It unwound like a shroud being removed. The painting, when he saw that that was what it was, made his breath catch in his throat. A girl smiled at him from the canvas. She was blonde, with clear green eyes; her skin was pale as dawn. Her pink silk dress was decorated with a brooch: a golden globe.

'Patience – it must be,' Paige whispered. She thrust the envelope towards him. 'Read it,' she said.

Curtis's hand shook as he took it from her. He cracked the red seal. A thick fold of paper slid out. He scanned it quickly, looking for the name at the bottom of the letter. 'It's from William, not Verity,' he said.

'What does it say?' Paige asked.

'Listen,

'"*Dear Maggie,*

'"*It is with a mixture of sadness and shame that I write to you now. A tragic event has taken place, the repercussions*

of which will surely stay with our families for many years. I know for my part that the loss I feel can hardly be borne.

"'My daughter, Patience, was taken from me. Your son, Christopher, was also taken from this world. They died moments apart. Your son acted with valour such has surprised and astonished us all.

"'Four days ago, Patience took it in mind to go boating upon the lake here with a party of friends. Christopher took the oars. Her friends tell us that when the boat reached the centre of the lake, Patience stood in an attempt to pick one of the lilies that grow there. What happened next is painful to relate, but I must do so. My daughter fell from the boat into the water. With great presence of mind and superlative courage, your son dived in to rescue her. Tragically, that attempt was in vain. Both she and he perished in the water. Their bodies were recovered, but life had left them.'"

Curtis stopped reading; he looked up at the room. The adults sat so still they were hardly breathing. Paige, next to him, had eyes that were damp with tears.

'Is that it?' she whispered.

'No, there's more.'

'Well, keep reading then!'

"'The cause of my shame will be obvious to you, madam. It was I who brought your son here. I took him from you as though he were a pet dog that I could do with as I wished.

I treated him as less than a man. Despite this, his bravery showed me that he was more than I could ever hope to be. He was a true friend to our family. A true friend to Patience. I am only sorry that I was less than a friend to him.

"'I cannot return your son to you. I should not have taken him from you. But I can promise you that your son will be held in high regard among my family for generations to come. Furthermore, his story shall be told amongst all the citizens here. In our darkness, we shall bring light.

"'Death masks have been taken of our children. I have commissioned two portraits to be painted from these likenesses.

"'The painting of your son will hang here in Wickworth Manor alongside the mask of Patience. Both will remain side by side, their memories cherished by my family.

"'The portrait of my daughter, and the mask of Christopher, I send to you along with this letter, that you may be reminded of the esteem in which your son will be held in his master's country.

"'In further recompense, I send a sum of money for yourself and your remaining family. This comes in addition to your family's freedom which I shall arrange with the foreman of my plantation. I am currently unwell and so I shall commission my remaining daughter, Verity, to see that all this is done.

"'I am no longer your master, though I wish to become,

"'Your friend,

"'William Burton'"

There was silence for a moment.

Then Paige said, 'She never knew. His mother never knew how brave he'd been. She never received her own freedom. Verity didn't send William's letter or the painting. She hid them instead. Why would someone do that?'

'She said in her letter,' Curtis said. 'If the real story got out, it would have been ammunition for the people fighting against slavery. People would have known that a slave had a mind and a will of their own and could be brave. Verity didn't want that to happen. Her fortune depended on it.'

'For all the good it did her.' It was Mrs Burton-Jones who had spoken. Curtis looked across at her, sitting in one of the armchairs. Her face was still, shocked; her hand rested on her chest. 'She died alone, you know. Not even her own servants with her. They were frightened of her. I heard the stories when I was a little girl.'

'What stories?' Paige asked.

Mrs Burton-Jones didn't seem to notice that it was Paige who'd asked the question. Her eyes were fixed on the painting. 'They said she was haunted by the Wickworth Boy. That he had cursed her. It seems it was the other way around; she cursed him. I should thank you,' she said, finally looking at Paige. 'You've uncovered a story that my family should have told a long time ago.'

Curtis felt Paige lean against his shoulder. She smelled of dust and shampoo. 'What now?' he asked. 'Are we being sent home?'

Miss Brown looked at Mrs Burton-Jones and raised one eyebrow. Mrs Burton-Jones shook her head. 'In the circumstances, I shouldn't think that's necessary, not unless you want to go.'

'No!' Curtis said. 'I don't want to leave.'

'Are you sure?' Mum asked.

'I'm staying here,' Curtis said.

'OK, but we're finding you a proper room to sleep in and that's final,' Mum said.

CHAPTER 34

October

Paige Owens turned over the tarot card and slapped it down on the back seat of the bus. 'The Star!' she said.

Curtis Okafor grinned. 'You know I'm not listening.'

'*I'm* listening,' Sal said. 'What does the Star mean?'

'It means recognition, success. You know, like making it through to the final round on *The X Factor*.'

'Is that what we've done?'

The bus pulled up outside an old building. It had lots of columns and big windows, like the bank in *Mary Poppins*. 'Neoclassical,' Paige said.

'Get you, Miss Know-it-all,' Curtis laughed.

Jo leaned over the seat in front. 'This is cool, you two being the guests of honour at the Museum. Isn't it, Liam?'

She nudged Liam, who was sitting beside her.

'Yeah. Cool,' he said.

Mr Appleton stood up at the front of the bus. 'Everyone, please remember that you are here representing Avon High School, so no nonsense. Go straight off the bus and through into the Main Hall.'

Paige and Curtis were the last to get off.

Curtis looked at her. 'You OK?' he asked. He was smiling slightly and his face was relaxed. It was good to see him happy.

Paige nodded firmly.

Inside the Museum, a curator was waiting to lead them into the exhibition hall. The room had been decorated to look like an eighteenth-century drawing room. Objects were arranged in cases, things that the museum had collected together over the last few months – a model of a ship like the one Christopher sailed on; brushes and combs used in the eighteenth century, all kinds of things that would tell people more about that time. In the centre of the exhibition, hung above a fake fireplace, were two paintings, side by side. Patience and Christopher.

Paige walked past the crowd of people towards the fireplace. The canvases had been cleaned and the two figures looked bright and full of life. Underneath, the museum curator had added a label:

CJTE/060 Two paintings, oil on canvas, artist unknown. 1805.

'Look,' Curtis said, joining her. 'The museum has written his story. Or rather they've guessed at his story. The label on the crew list says he got seasick on the way, and that one says he heard about a runaway slave.'

'Can they really know that, do you think?'

He shrugged. 'I don't know. But stuff like that would have happened to *someone*, even if it wasn't Christopher. So it's kind of true, isn't it?'

Paige looked up at the portrait of the Wickworth Boy, at Christopher, one last time. His eyes were as fierce as ever, but the cleaning of the surface had revealed something new, something like a smile.

The curator began speaking from a portable stage near the window. 'I'm Veronique Bernard. We are delighted to host this exhibition, which will travel on to the West Indies later in the year. These paintings and the surviving letters shed light on one of the most intriguing artefacts in the Fitzgerald Archive . . .'

The speech went on for a while. Paige looked at the model of a ship in the glass case next to her, imagining it being tossed and thrown by a stormy sea.

'You know,' Curtis whispered, 'there still isn't the

tiniest scrap of evidence that Patience and Christopher were in love.'

Paige sighed. It was awful to have to admit that Curtis was right about something, but he did have a point. 'Nothing except the stories,' she said.

'They're just stories though.'

'Good stories.'

He nodded. 'Do you remember that first day we met and you told me about a ghost who haunted the place looking for his lost love? Out seeking revenge?'

She nodded. 'We put his spirit to rest. Mum said so.'

'Maybe we did, in a way,' Curtis agreed. 'But I'm afraid that without any proof of them being in love, you still owe me a Curly Wurly.'

CJTE/060 Two paintings, oil on canvas, artist unknown. 1805.

Christopher did not know if he would ever see his home again. He had left it hoping for a new life, a new freedom. But although the landscape around him had changed, the rules that bound him did not. Possibly he would have been aware of stirrings of reform as the voices against the slave trade grew stronger. In the courts, the law was tested. But there would have been no way for Christopher to know what the future would hold. He would have faced that without certainty - as we all do.

AUTHOR'S NOTE

The painting that Curtis and Paige discover in the story was inspired by a real painting. Called 'A Negro Coachboy', it is an eighteenth-century painting of a boy who lived in North Wales. Almost nothing is known about the life of that boy. I saw the painting often when I was growing up and I always wanted to know more about him. That was going to be impossible, so, instead, I imagined a story for him.

I learned a lot while researching the story. For example, I discovered that estimates put the number of black people living in Britain during the late eighteenth century at around 10,000. I also found out that there was a lot of confusion around whether slave ownership was legal in Britain at all. Some people living then believed that a decision by the courts in 1772 (the Somerset ruling) made slavery illegal, but, in fact, it was not that simple and the practice continued for a long time after that. It continues in some forms to this day.

The original painting is from the first half of the eighteenth century, but I took liberties and made Christopher live after the Somerset ruling was made.

I can't know what life was like for a slave living in Britain more than two hundred years ago, but I hope that the boy in the painting would be happy that people are thinking about him so long after his death.

ABOUT THE AUTHOR

Elen Caldecott graduated with an MA in Writing for Young People from Bath Spa University. Before becoming a writer, she was an archaeologist, a nurse, a theatre usher and a museum security guard. It was while working at the museum that Elen realised there is a way to steal anything if you think about it hard enough. Elen either had to become a master thief, or create some characters to do it for her – and so her debut novel, *How Kirsty Jenkins Stole the Elephant*, was born. It was shortlisted for the Waterstones Children's Prize and was followed by *How Ali Ferguson Saved Houdini* and *Operation Eiffel Tower*. Elen lives in Bristol with her husband, Simon, and their dog.

www.elencaldecott.com

Check out the **Elen Caldecott Children's Author**
page on Facebook

GET CREATIVE WITH
ELEN'S AWESOME ADVENTURE AWARD

TO CELEBRATE ALL YOUR WONDERFUL ADVENTURES AND TO SHOW YOUR CREATIVE SIDE, WE WANT YOU TO MAKE YOUR VERY OWN ADVENTURE COLLAGE.

YOUR ADVENTURE CAN RANGE FROM A TRIP TO THE ZOO TO A HOLIDAY IN JAPAN, AND YOUR COLLAGE CAN BE AS BIG OR SMALL AS YOU WISH!

SEND YOUR ENTRY TO US AND YOU WILL BE IN WITH A CHANCE OF WINNING SOME FANTASTIC PRIZES, WHICH INCLUDE:

- A FULL, SIGNED SET OF ELEN CALDECOTT'S BOOKS
- £100 OF TOPSHOP VOUCHERS
- AN IPOD TOUCH TO TAKE ON YOUR NEXT ADVENTURE

THE WINNING ENTRY WILL FEATURE ON THE WEBSITE!

FOR MORE INFORMATION ON HOW TO ENTER, CLOSING DATES, AND TERMS AND CONDITIONS, VISIT:

WWW.ELENSAWESOMEADVENTURES.COM